E. LYNN HARRIS

NOT A DAY GOES BY

E. Lynn Harris is the author of ten other novels and the memoir *What Becomes of the Broken-hearted*. His novels *Just Too Good to Be True*, *I Say a Little Prayer*, *A Love of My Own*, and *Any Way the Wind Blows* hit the bestseller lists in the *New York Times*, the *Wall Street Journal*, the *Washington Post*, and other publications. Harris died in 2009.

www.elynnharris.com

ANCHOR BOOKS

A Division of Random House, Inc.

New York

NOT A DAY GOES BY

A NOVEL

E. LYNN HARRIS

Second Anchor Books Edition, January 2004

This novel is a work of fiction. Any resemblance to real events,
businesses, organizations, and locales are intended only to give the
fiction a sense of reality and authenticity. Any resemblance to actual
persons, living or dead, is entirely coincidental.

The Library of Congress has cataloged the Doubleday edition as follows:
Harris, E. Lynn.
Not a day goes by: a novel / by E. Lynn Harris.—1st ed.
p. cm.
ISBN 0-385-49824-1
1. Separation (Psychology)—Fiction. I. Title.
PS3558.A64438 N68 2000
813'.54—dc21 00-38368

Anchor ISBN: 1-4000-7578-5

www.anchorbooks.com

Printed in the United States of America
10 9 8 7

THE AUTHOR THANKS . . .

Thiis author is grateful for my personal savior, the Lord Jesus Christ, for his daily blessing and the knowledge that I could not do this alone.

This author thanks his family, all of them, but most especially my mother, Etta W. Harris, my aunt, Jessie L. Phillips, and Rodrick L. Smith for being my rock and source of inspiration.

This author thanks his friends, both old and new . . . Lencola Sullivan, Vanessa Gilmore, Robin Walters, Cindy Barnes, Debra Martin Chase, Troy Danato, Dyanna Williams, Anthony Bell, Bruce Fuller, Carlton Brown, Kevin Edwards, Martha K. Levin, Yolanda Starks, Sybil Wilkes, Brent Zachery, Anderson Phillips, Tavis Smiley, Regina Daniels, Rose Crater Hamilton, Tracey and David Huntley, Christopher Martin, Derrick Thompson, Deborah Crable, and Brian Chandler.

This author thanks Doubleday (which has the best suits

in the business) for being a company that not only publishes great books but also cares about the people who write them . . . Steve Rubin, Michael Palgon, Jackie Everly, Mario Pulice, Roberta Spivak, Suzanne Herz, Alison Rich, and Bill Thomas. Special thanks to Eleanor Branch and Jenny Frost at Random House Audio.

This author thanks his support team (manager, agents, lawyers, and accountant) . . . Laura Gilmore, John Hawkins, Moses Cardona, Irv Schwartz, Amy Goldsend, and Bob Braunschweig.

This author thanks his editors, who all happen to be talented writers and great friends as well . . . Charles Flowers, Dellanor Young, and Rosalind Oliphant.

This author thanks all the booksellers and the ones who are wonderful friends as well . . . Blanche Richardson, Desiree Sanders, Garbo Hearne, Emma Rodgers, Clara Villarosa, Michelle Lewis, Antoine and Theresa Coffer, and Sherry McGee.

This author thanks some special people and organizations that make him always look good . . . Jen Marshall, Shannon Jones, Tarus Sorrells, Janis Murray, Sherri Steinfield, Matthew Jordan Smith, Lloyd Boston, *Code* magazine, *Essence Magazine, The Tom Joyner Morning Show, The Doug Banks Show, The Mod Squad,* Frank Ski and his morning team, Ryan Cameron and his team, the NAACP, Delta Sigma Theta, Alpha Kappa Alpha, Zeta Phi Beta, The Links, *The Donnie Simpson Show,* and *SBC Magazine.*

This author thanks the staff of Trump International Hotel for making it a dream place to write. Thanks also to the colleges and universities which extended kind invitations followed by very warm receptions.

This author thanks Robert Bass, former football great from the University of Miami, for friendship and inside information on agents and football, which helped this novel greatly.

This author thanks the University of Arkansas football team for winning the 2000 Cotton Bowl (with apologies to all the Texas Longhorn fans), the track team for winning the National Championship . . . again, and the *puppies* aka the Razorback Basketball team for winning the SEC tournament. *I can't wait till next year, Mr. Nolan Richardson!*

This author thanks all his writer friends who make me proud to be a writer and those who have offered wonderful advice and friendship . . . Iyanla Vanzant, Terry McMillan, R. M. Johnson, Yolanda Joe, Eric Jerome Dickey, Bebe Moore Campbell, Nathan McCall, LaJoyce Warlick, Tina McElroy Ansa, Tananarive Due, Brian Keith Jackson, and Walter Mosley.

This author thanks and is grateful daily for my senior editor at Doubleday, the amazing Janet Hill.

And finally, this author thanks you, the reader, for all your continued love and support.

Until next time . . . e. lynn harris . . . Chicago, Illinois

PART ONE

BASIL WAS certain. After a couple of sleepless nights, he was more certain than he had been about anything in his life. There was nothing more for him to do but to inform the person most affected by his decision, his bride to be, Broadway star Yancey Harrington Braxton.

It was the last Sunday of the century. A perfect day for a winter wedding. New York City was bone-chillingly cold, with a new coat of snow. The fierceness of winter had arrived and the city looked white and felt gray.

John Basil Henderson gazed at the phone on the massive, leather-topped desk in his midtown hotel suite and then at the gold monogrammed cuff links Yancey had presented to him after their engagement party. His eyes glanced at the large gold ring on his right hand, a treasured token from his football days. He was only half dressed, wearing black pants, socks, and an eggshell-white silk T-shirt.

Basil moved a few steps, heaved a deep sigh and picked up the phone, pressed the button labeled opera- tor, and when the chirpy young female voice said, "How can I help you, Mr. Henderson?" Basil paused for a mo- ment and responded, "Can you ring 2619, Ms. Braxton's suite?"

"I'll be happy to," she replied. Before she put the call through she added, "Congratulations, Mr. Henderson."

Basil was startled for a moment. "Congratulations? For what?"

"You are the Mr. Henderson who's getting married to- day, right? I saw your name on the ballroom schedule. The room looks beautiful. Decorated like a winter won- derland."

"Yeah. Thank you."

After a few computerized beeps, Yancey answered the phone with a voice filled with joy.

"Yancey," Basil said.

"Baby! I thought it would be Oscar. You know, the guy who's going to do my hair, or maybe Sam, who's doing my makeup. Are you ready? Can you believe we'll be married before the evening is over? I've waited so long for this day," Yancey rambled as she played with her hair in front of a full-length mirror in her flower-filled suite.

A few seconds of silence passed before Basil said, "I can't do it."

"Can't do what? Basil, baby . . . what are you talking about? What can't you do?"

"I can't marry you," he said calmly. His voice was cool and controlled.

"What!" she screamed. This was not happening,

Yancey told herself as she pressed her hand to her forehead. Wearing an off-white satin slip, she sat down on the bed in a state of shock, her mind closing down, refusing to comprehend Basil's words.

"Yancey, calm down," Basil advised.

"'Calm down,' mutherfucker, have you lost your mind? Well, of course you have. What other kind of fool would do this to somebody?" Yancey said without taking a breath.

"Yancey, this kind of talk isn't going to solve anything. I've made up my mind and that's that."

"'That's that?' That's all you got to say to me? All my guests are getting ready to come to *my* wedding, the wedding my mother has been planning since the time you asked me to marry you, and you give me some 'that's that' bullshit? I don't think so!" Yancey said as she lifted her body from the bed. Her sable-brown eyes flooded instantly with tears of rage and humiliation.

"What about all the press that's going to be here? I'll be the laughingstock of New York," she added.

"Yancey, I'm going to say this for the last time and then I'm going to hang up. I can't marry you."

"But why?" Yancey asked faintly. The tone of her voice had changed in seconds from forceful to pleading.

"Yancey, you know why," Basil said firmly.

While dabbing away her tears, somewhere in Yancey's heart she knew exactly why her dream wedding could never take place.

MY LADY, Yancey, changed my life. Sometimes I think she saved my life. My name is John Basil Henderson and I guess I'm what you call a former bad boy. I was the kind of dude who was getting so much play, I needed to buy condoms by the barrel. About two years ago, all that changed when I met Yancey Harrington Braxton the day before Christmas at Rockefeller Center while skating with my five-year-old nephew, Cade. Yancey walked right up and started a conversation while flirting with both Cade and myself. I loved her confidence. We were both smitten at her first hello. Yancey is, as the young dudes would say, a "dime piece" . . . a perfect ten.

When I met Yancey I was in the midst of a pre-midlife crisis. I had just turned thirty-three and my childhood dream of playing pro football was already over. Wasn't shit going right for me. I was actually seeing a shrink, trying to figure out why I had such disdain for both men and women while, at times, being sexually attracted to both. I was spending too much time trying to get even with this mofo, Raymond Tyler, who didn't even know how strongly I felt about him. For me, Raymond stood on that thin line between love and hate. There were so many things I liked—no, *loved*—about him, but I also hated feeling that way toward any man. It just wasn't right.

I had gone to the doctor to face my past—a past that included my sexual molestation by a much beloved uncle. I wrote that no good mofo a letter telling him how he had screwed up my life with his sick ass, but the mofo died before I could mail it. I was surprised at how writing shit down and talking out loud about how I was feeling helped me. But the good doctor wasn't excited about my relationship with Yancey, and when I disagreed, we parted ways. It wasn't as if he said, "If you continue in the relationship I can no longer see you, Mr. Henderson." I just stopped going and he never called to see if I was okay. I guess he didn't need the money.

There have been times in my life that were so painful that I didn't think I could share them with another living soul, but then that person walks into your life, and you don't know whether to be afraid or feel relief. You don't know whether to run or stand still. That was the way I felt about meeting Yancey. When I told her how my father had raised me to believe that my mother was dead, which I later found out was a total lie, Yancey held me tight and I felt her tears on my naked shoulder. At times I feel as though I could tell her anything, and then I remember she is a woman and wouldn't understand some of the things I have been through and done. So, despite my bone-deep love for Yancey, I've kept some secrets about myself she just wouldn't understand.

My love for Yancey hit me hard. I guess that's the way real love works. I love the way she makes me feel like I'm the only man in a roomful of thousands. I love the way other men and women look at us when we walk hand in hand into some of New York's finest restaurants and nightclubs, or during our simple walks through Central Park. I love watching her perform on the Broadway stage and in cabarets, where Yancey charms both owners and patrons. I love the sound of her singing, not only on stage but in the bathroom, while she sits at her vanity and brushes her hair.

But one of the things I love the most about Yancey is she reminds me of myself. I guess both of us have taken so much shit from our families that we don't take too kindly to outsiders. We are each other's best friend. To the outside world we're the diva and the dawg, but not with each other. Once I took her to Athens, Georgia, for a college football game. After the game we went to a sports bar for beer and chicken wings. The redheaded waitress with colossal breasts was diggin' me. When she served us, ole girl bent down so low I could smell her deodorant. Yancey definitely took note. So when the waitress did one more dip and looked me directly in the eyes and asked, "Can I git anything else for y'all?" Yancey stood up and said, "Yes, you can git them fake titties out of my man's face." That's my Yancey. Another time, shortly after we first started dating and I was still keeping a few freaks on the side, Yancey came over to spend the night. I came out of the shower expecting to see her lying in my bed wearing something sexy, but she was fully dressed. When I asked her what was up, she told me, "I don't sleep in no bed where I can smell another woman's perfume or pussy." I got the message.

I had a gig doing sportscasting for a network, and when I became fed up with the way they were treating me, Yancey convinced me that I could do better. As we talked one evening while enjoying a late supper, I realized I wanted a business that combined my love for sports and making money. A couple of weeks later a former team-mate called me looking for additional capital to expand his small sports management agency. I hadn't heard from Brison Tucker since the night the two of us went out and got messed up big time after we were both chosen in the first round of the NFL draft. Brison was injured after four years in the league, and had spent several years working in Canada as a scout. A couple of long dinners and months later, I was no longer a talking head at ESPN do-ing second-rate college games but a partner of XJI (X Jocks Inc.), one of the fastest-growing sports agencies in the country, with offices in New York, Washington, D.C., and Atlanta, with over thirty employees. The agency is looking to add another partner and open offices in Chicago and Los Angeles.

Joining the XJI was the right move at the right time. I had made some decent money with Internet stocks and was looking for another investment. Instead of just hand-ing over money, I joined the firm as a partner. This year alone, XJI has six potential number-one picks in the up-coming NFL draft as well as four NBA lottery picks. I personally signed three of the players. The agency also has a couple of NBA superstars who left their white agents and signed with us, as well as a couple of WNBA players and some track and field hardheads. I love what I do, and I've rekindled some old friendships with my partners and made new friends with some of the players I represent. I feel a certain power when I make big-money deals for my clients, especially since the money is coming from wealthy owners who view the players as possessions. If these rich mofos want to play with my players, then I make sure they pay major benjamins.

As for me, myself, and I? We're rollin' like a bowling ball! I recently purchased a penthouse loft on Lafayette Street with twenty-six-foot-high ceilings and wood-burning fireplaces in both the living room and the master bedroom. I got a closetful of finely tailored suits and I could go months without wearing the same pair of draws or socks. Yancey and I take vacations in places like Jamaica, Fisher Island, and Paris whenever New York becomes too much of a grind. I'm doing better than I ever did when I was playing professional football.

Still, the biggest change in my life is the way I feel about women. With the love of Yancey and my sister, Campbell, I have come to view women differently for the very first time. I didn't know I had a sister until two years ago, just before I met Yancey. Turns out my mom had remarried and on her deathbed told Campbell she had a brother. She tracked me down, and suddenly I had two new women in my life. Before, I'd never have let women get that close to me.

In Campbell I see a woman determined to give her son, Cade, and husband, Hewitt, the best she has to offer. Sometimes I just like to watch her with Cade, feeding him french fries or making sure his coat is buttoned up before he goes out into the cold. I love the way she smiles and hugs him whenever he comes into a room, even when he's only been gone for a short time.

There was a time in my life when I had a lot of anger toward women. I put them in two categories: whores and sluts. The only difference is, a whore gives up the sex because she wants something material, whereas a slut just loves the sex. I have been with both, but I didn't like the power pussy had over me. Maybe my anger toward women happened because I grew up without a mother, or because I simply hadn't met the right woman. Now, thanks to Yancey and Campbell, I no longer view them as a resting place for my manhood but a place where I can rest my heart. Now don't get me wrong, I ain't *whipped* and I'm not ready for the choir robe and halo. I still got my tough-guy swagger (when needed). The only difference between two years ago and today is I realize that a tough-guy swagger looks just as dumb as a robe and halo.

YANCEY Harrington Braxton was as complicated as she was beautiful. A woman from Jackson, Tennessee, who never felt she belonged in a small town, Yancey came to New York when she was twenty-two years old. In less than two years, she had made a name for herself with her triple threat skills of being able to act, sing, and dance with the best of Broadway's veteran divas. But Yancey wasn't satisfied with leading roles in several Broadway shows. She perfected her skills by taking private lessons in acting, dance, and voice from the best New York had to offer. When Yancey wasn't in class, she was in the gym making sure her body remained flawless. It was only a matter of time, Yancey thought, before she would take these talents and body to Hollywood and exceed even her wildest childhood dreams.

A statuesque five feet eight, 115 pounds, with a twenty-two-inch waist, Yancey walked with the grace of a haughty runway model. Actually she didn't just walk into a room, she sauntered. Shoulders back, chest out, Miss America smile. And always, as if preparing to take a bow, she would carefully pan a room, sizing up her audience's impression of her.

Yancey imagined herself a beige princess, but through the eyes of others, she was a brilliant bronze. A century ago, she would have been considered just brown enough for the big house, but much too brown to pass. You could tell she was black. No cream in the coffee going on there.

Yancey was one of those women who still believed women with long tresses had an advantage, so she kept her hair long and had extensions added. Her lush, chemically treated and colored hair was a dusky auburn that fell just below her shoulders. She loved the versatility of her hair—ponytails (which she loved), french rolls (when she wanted to look regal), upsweeps, and ringlets. Yancey loved to experiment with the styles in fashion magazines. One of her most striking features was her thick eyebrows, which were always seductively and precisely arched.

In high school, she was the kind of person who wrote long, elaborate passages in the yearbooks of her classmates, but wouldn't remember their names a week later when she would bump into them in the mall or class. Instead of attending her ten-year class reunion, Yancey had sent press packets with her full-color head shots and "Best wishes" scribbled under her signature, a well-studied signature she had practiced since the moment she learned to write her name at age six.

Yancey lived on the Upper East Side in an exclusive 2700-square-foot townhouse, which included a studio/library and servant's quarters. She had bought the plush home with funds inherited from her grandmother's life insurance policy and from the sale of her Jackson, Tennessee, home and some land her grandmother owned in Mississippi. There were times between jobs when Yancey had a tough time paying the mortgage, yet somehow she always managed. Just when things were getting tight with the pocketbook, Yancey would land a national commercial or get a gig singing backup for major pop acts. She liked the recording jobs, since she was not only making a little extra cash but also picking up tips for the day someone would be singing backup for her.

Even though her financial situation sometimes became very dire, Yancey was a diva's diva and refused to waitress or do temp work like many of her Broadway peers. And above all, she could not bring herself to file for unemployment when a show or job ended.

In the close-knit world of New York entertainment, Yancey was known as the replacement queen. She had stepped into many leading roles on Broadway when established actresses took vacation or suddenly fell ill. Yancey had performed in *The Lion King, Rent, Chicago, Smokey Joe's Café,* and was currently appearing in *Fosse.*

These shows added not only to her bank account but also to her reputation as a talented performer who could play the virginal beauty and belt out a soul-stirring gospel tune as well. Still, Yancey was not satisfied. She hated the fact that the only time a call came was to replace an actress of color, and she was pressing not only her agent but producers as well to consider her for roles with nontraditional casting. If it happened for Vanessa L. Williams and Audra MacDonald, then it could happen for her.

Often she would scour the pages of *Backstage* and *Variety* looking for roles that didn't match any of her characteristics. Burdened with the fear of being labeled racist, flustered directors and producers had no choice but to allow the talented beauty to at least audition for the roles. Once, when she had the chance to replace a Hispanic actress on a soap opera in a recurring role, Yancey quit before she signed a contract because she thought the work was not only beneath her but too little for too much in terms of compensation. The only thing Yancey daydreamed of constantly was a starring role either on Broadway or in a film, or a recording contract that she could put her mark on, and if a Tony, Grammy, Emmy, or Oscar followed, well, that would be just the way things were supposed to be.

And now Yancey figured she had hit the jackpot in the man department. When she met Basil, she thought at the very least he would be a good roll in the sheets, especially when she caught a glimpse of him bending over to help his nephew at the Rockefeller Center skating rink. Basil was a wall of muscle: a strong-shouldered man, with a barrel chest, a six-pack stomach, all spread like Italian silk over a six-foot-four frame. When he turned around and smiled in her direction, Yancey thought he was so achingly handsome with his catlike gray eyes, she couldn't help but think of him completely naked with his huge arms wrapped around her. His was a body she wanted to see up close and personal. Yet she made him wait almost six months for that pleasure when she discovered there was more to Basil than an amazing body. Yancey found him to be a brother with expensive taste and a wallet to back up her desire for the finer things in life.

She found Basil a sensitive man who had survived a dysfunctional childhood somewhat similar to her own. Yancey had been raised by her grandmother, while her mother, Ava, traveled the world in search of a career as an entertainer. She had never laid eyes on her father. Yancey had followed in her mother's footsteps and, after her grandmother died, mother and daughter had forged a tentative friendship that was more like a difficult sibling relationship than a mother-daughter bond. Ava had never been there for Yancey when she really needed her for emotional support, and it seemed that whenever Yancey had a little problem she needed to talk over with her mother, Ava had a bigger one. So Yancey had come to accept that all she could really expect from her mother was lively and entertaining conversation and occasional monetary support in the form of a check sent via overnight mail whenever Yancey was between jobs. When Basil asked Yancey if that bothered her, she replied, with a hint of Southern lushness in a voice that she had tried to rid herself of, "It's all I've ever known." She always felt the toughness developed in her childhood served her well in her show business aspirations, as well as her outlook on love and life. When it came to show business, Yancey often told herself she was looking for awards, not friends.

Years ago, after her first adult relationship with Derrick, her college sweetheart, had ended badly, she promised herself to never fall in love too deeply. So Yancey loved Basil in her own way. Whenever they kissed, she told Basil how much she loved him, but there was always a little voice whispering inside her head that it's okay to love, but never too hard, or too much.

1

SO WHERE you headed this weekend?" I asked as I dried my hair with a plush white towel.

"I'm going to Gainesville for the Florida-Tennessee game. What about yourself?" Nico Benson asked as he wiped his tall and broad-shouldered body. As business partners, we often checked in with each other on who had the crazier schedule.

"I'm doing Arkansas-Alabama. Should be a great game," I said. I reached into my gym locker and pulled out the new pair of black underwear I had bought on Fifth Avenue the day before.

"What players are you looking at?" Nico asked, putting on some light-blue cotton boxers.

"Lucus from Arkansas and Alexander from 'Bama," I said.

It was the third Wednesday in September. Once a month, my partners and I would take the entire office for a free day to release the tensions in the competitive world of sports management. This month we had decided on a day at the Chelsea Piers Sports Center. We had started the morning with breakfast, played basketball, and then had individual spa treatments like facials and massages. Our senior partner and president, Brison Tucker, had already showered and headed to the office for work. There was no way for Brison, a chronic workaholic, to fully understand the meaning of what a free day meant. After lunch, Nico and I had played a couple of games of racquetball.

Nico, a peanut-brown brother who talked more smack than a gum-chewing truck stop waitress, was drying his body from his shower as I put on my sexy see-through underwear. Nico had played basketball at Duke and for a couple of years in the NBA in Vancouver and Houston. He was only twenty-seven and was a great asset to our firm because he was smart and could still relate on a personal basis to the young athletes we were pursuing. In a lot of ways Nico reminded me of my former self.

I was pulling my slacks out of my locker when suddenly Nico's dark brown eyes swept sideways. "Dude," he whispered, "do you know that guy? He's sweatin' you big time."

I turned in the direction of Nico's eyes and ended up looking dead in the face of a squash-yellow, overweight dude with his tongue hanging out, his eyes bulging in disbelief. This was no big shock to me. I was used to people staring at me longer than what was socially acceptable. Especially when I was naked. My ass was perfect and my jimmie was both long and thick. It had been known to make both women and grown men weep. I'm not arrogant, just honest. Even when I was only semi-hard, my jimmie hung perfectly still. Sometimes I enjoyed the attention, but not in locker rooms and not when I was with a Mister Macho-Macho like Nico. So with a stern face I looked at the dumpy-looking brother and asked, "Do I know you?"

A blank expression covered his face before he mumbled, "No." He looked like he was frozen with fear.

"Then why in the fuck are you all in my grill, or should I say in my draws?" I demanded. I felt my anger rising. Why couldn't these gay mofos leave me alone? Didn't they know I wasn't playing on *their* team anymore?

After a few uncomfortable seconds he asked awkwardly, "I was wondering where you got that underwear from." I looked down at the tight-fitting black silk underwear that felt like a breath caressing my ass and then at my admirer. "Don't worry about it. They don't make them in your size, you faggot mutherfucker." I turned around and looked at Nico, who smiled, and we gave each other a tap with our hands balled.

"Man, a straight brother ain't safe nowhere with all these faggots around," Nico said.

"True . . . true. But I let 'em know right up front I'm the wrong one to fuck with," I said as I grabbed my gym bag and shut my locker.

LATER that evening, I was killing time reviewing tapes of some of the players I was hoping to sign with the firm. I was going to meet Yancey at a restaurant in the theater district after her show. This was the last week for Yancey in *Fosse* and I felt she needed me there for moral support. But after about ten times I was *Fosseed* out, so meeting her right after her performance was the next best thing.

I went to the kitchen to get a beer when the incident at the gym popped into my head. I try not to act uptight around gay guys, but they seemed to be getting more forward than I can *ever* remember. Now some of them will just come up and ask for the beef. With Yancey being in the theater, where she is surrounded by gay men, I always have my guard up.

One time I came close to getting busted about my past. The producers of *Fosse* threw a party for Yancey when she joined the cast. Yancey and I were front and center enjoying the attention, when who walks in but this dude I used to pump, Monty Johnson. He was a has-been R&B singer who was now doing background vocals and trying to break into Broadway. We made eye contact and while Yancey was accepting praise from her new castmates, I went over to shake Monty's hand and say whas-sup to ole boy. I knew I needed to get to him before he bounced over to speak to me in front of Yancey. I didn't need any *how do you know him* questions from Yancey. She wasn't like a lot of sistahs who never thought of dudes kickin' it with each other. She knew threats could come in both the male and female form.

After saying hello, I realized Monty was acting real cool, too cool, like I was just somebody he spoke to at the gym or walking down the street. I guess he had forgotten how good the dick used to be. He quickly introduced me to his buddy, a tall and lean guy sporting a pierced tongue and his hair styled in jailhouse cornrows. They were giggling with each other like two teenage girls at the stage door of their favorite boy group. When ole boy left to get Monty a drink, Monty told me he was in love and was sorry about any misunderstanding our last visit had caused me. When I told him I was in love, and who the lucky lady was, he smiled and whispered, "You always did like the ladies more. But from what I've heard about Miss Diva Deluxe Yancey, you might have met your match." Before I could ask him what he meant, I caught a glimpse of Yancey looking in my direction, so I hauled ass over toward her.

Monty was the culprit who had ended my last serious relationship with a woman. I was dating a sister named Yolanda, who walked in on us while I had Monty ass up across my sofa. After that fiasco and a few other missteps, I came up with my own little list of rules to keep me from courting temptation.

I call them "Basil's Rules to Keep the Knuckleheads Away from the Family Jewels." Some of the do's and don'ts are obvious, like not going to gay bars, cruising parks, or smiling at male flight attendants, but those don't apply to me since I never did any of those things. The rules are: Avoid men who try to make eye contact with you or men who can't because they're looking at your crotch. Don't go to the gym during rush hour, which could mean early morning or right after work. This is hard to follow since gay men are at the gym when the door opens and when it closes. I don't know where they come from. Sometimes it seems as though they are dropping from the ceiling butt-ass naked, shaving, pissing, and trying to strike up a conversation. Don't let anybody spot you while lifting weights unless you're paying them. Keep away from men who have complete sets of designer luggage. Avoid mofos with colored contacts, especially yellow boys with green contacts and dark guys with sky-blue contacts. Stay out of churches with large choirs. Avoid dudes who wear shirts that look more like maternity dresses or men with extended music (usually Diana Ross or Patti LaBelle) on their answering machines; mofos who wear their sweaters or jackets around the waist; men who, in their conversations, use the word "lover" when discussing their significant other; men with cats or small dogs, especially any type of fluffy Asian dog; men who frown at the suggestion of two hunnies making love and letting you watch; and finally, any woman, no matter how beautiful, who has hands bigger than yours.

2

FOR YANCEY, the prestige of things took precedence over her own preference. The address of her Upper East Side brownstone was really false advertising that she was an entertainer well paid for her talents. The furnishings and appointments she chose for her "diva domain" (as she liked to call her spacious living quarters) were more than a step above the budget of a Broadway actress. They were a kangaroo leap.

The first things visitors would notice were the foyer's marble floor, the glittering chandelier hanging above, and the antique coffee table with a tarnished silver top accented with an expensive-looking Chinese vase. But on guided tours, Yancey would first take her guests to the dance studio, her absolute favorite place to show. The studio and her bedroom were the only two rooms where she banished her decorator and let her soul dictate the design rather than her desire to impress.

In the studio, the overhead track lighting bounced off two mirrored walls, making the room appear much larger than it was. The shining maple wood floors and ballet barre enhanced a room that Yancey had always dreamed of since she took her first dance class back in Jackson. Hours seemed like minutes when she was in the room singing and dancing to music generated by her state-of-the-art sound system. *It is simply magical,* Yancey thought.

The room had been a library for the previous owner. When the contractor came to make a bid for the renovation, he convinced Yancey to keep at least one of the walls' splendidly built bookshelves. She agreed only after considering that one day there would be books written about her to fill the shelves. Until then, her collection of coffee table books on music and the theater filled the shelves. Yancey added a little texture to the shelves with memorabilia like dried flowers from her opening nights, and scented candles. In the corner of the room was a StairMaster and a pair of ten-pound free weights for those rainy days when Yancey didn't leave the house, not even for her gym time.

The living room was beautifully decorated with matching plum sofas and a coffee table covered with *Harper's Bazaar, Essence,* and her favorite, *Vanity Fair*. She had limited the amount of furniture in the room in order to create a warm and inviting space.

As far as Yancey was concerned, her bedroom was off limits to everyone but Basil. She was proud of its elegance and reveled in seeing the faces of the rare visitors she allowed to partake of its beauty. Once she had invited some young girls she had met at the Broadway Dance Center over for tea. Besides asking for her autograph and photos, they had impressed Yancey by telling her they had seen every show she had appeared in. One of the young ladies, a talented ballet dancer from the Bronx, had broken into tears when she wandered into Yancey's bedroom. She placed her hand over her mouth and whispered to Yancey, "This is the bedroom I see in my dreams." The rich cherrywood antiques may have been too formal for some, but for Yancey it was an opportunity to live out one of her *I am a princess* fantasies.

The queenly bed boasted four regal high posts. The armoire, vanity, and chest of drawers were carefully arranged, adding to the splendor of the room. Because the furniture's color and bulk were so heavy, Yancey chose soft pastel fabrics to give the room balance. Her duvet, bed ruffle, and drapes were ivory damask. Filling her linen closet were 350-thread-count cotton sheets in beautiful colors of lavender, peach, mint green, and sky blue. Four big lace-edged pillows were propped in front of the two small pillows dressed in the colored linen of the day.

A nightstand graced each side of the bed. Fragrant candles, fabric-covered boxes, and crystal bowls of potpourri sat atop each table. The table on the side where she slept held a telephone and a silver-framed photograph of Basil, looking handsome as usual. On the wall that greeted her each morning was an ode to Yancey. She had carefully arranged photos of herself in various shows and framed magazine covers from *In Theater, Playbill, The Paper,* and *Interview,* when Yancey had adorned each magazine as cover girl. There were spaces anxiously awaiting the covers from *People, Ebony,* and of course, *Vanity Fair*.

The room itself was painted in a soft gold. There was a corn-yellow leather chaise lounge covered with several dolls and stuffed animals. The hallway between the master bedroom, living room, and servant's quarters was a sea of chocolate walls covered with *Playbills* from Broadway shows and beautiful paintings by Deborah Roberts and Paul Goodnight. Yancey's penchant for tidiness, as well as the maid's biweekly visits, ensured her domain sparkled brighter than any star in the heavens.

For over a year, Yancey had had a roommate to help with the cost of her townhouse and expensive tastes. She had run an ad in *Backstage* and *New York,* but the applicants were beautiful up-and-coming divas and a couple of gay men. Yancey wasn't having any part of that, so she was happy when someone she vaguely knew came back into her life.

Windsor Louisa Adams was a broadly built woman, about five seven and 165 pounds, with reddish-brown medium dreads framing her plain nut-brown face. Windsor had met her when Yancey transferred from Vanderbilt University to Howard University and moved onto the same dorm floor. The two weren't close friends, because Yancey didn't let other women get too close, but they had been in a couple of university theater productions and had once organized a Christmas party for an old folks' home near the campus. But the only thing it seemed they had in common was that each had legally changed their middle names. Yancey changed her middle name from Elizabeth to Harrington after her favorite character from the movie *All About Eve*. Windsor just made a small alteration to her birth middle name of Louise, changing it to Louisa.

Windsor was not considered beautiful by most standards, but she ruled Howard University with her mesmerizing personality. She was president of the dorm, the number-one tennis player, and Homecoming Queen her junior year. The last time Yancey had seen Windsor was at a Greek show after she had pledged Delta Sigma Theta. She had even tried to get Yancey to pledge, but Yancey said she wasn't interested in joining a sorority because she thought sisterhood would go right out the window the first time some soror's boyfriend looked at Yancey longer than a minute. Windsor didn't know Yancey had been turned down for membership in another sorority, Alpha Kappa Alpha. Yancey was so crushed that she moved off campus with her boyfriend, Derrick.

When Windsor greeted her at the stage door when she was performing in *Chicago*, Yancey assumed she was just another fan. She startled Yancey when she raced up and gave her a big hug and said, "Honey, you worked that stage! You were the best one and this is a long way from some of our HU productions."

Windsor had put on a little weight since college, and she no longer sported the long, layered hairstyle with hazel contacts. She realized Yancey didn't remember her, so Windsor reminded Yancey of the night they had sung a duet at the annual spring talent show. "Remember? We sang 'Enough Is Enough' and wore them out!"

"You're from Detroit, right?" Yancey asked, finally remembering the overly friendly dorm mate.

"Yeah, that's right. Remember, my mother used to send me fried chicken and coconut cakes in the mail and I used to share them with the floor?"

"Oh yeah," Yancey said as she looked Windsor up and down, thinking her mother must still be sending her food through the mail.

After a few minutes, Windsor suggested they go for a cup of coffee and talk about their days at Howard. When Yancey resisted, saying she needed her rest, Windsor simply locked her arms in Yancey's, gave her a big smile, and said, "I won't keep you out that long."

Over coffee and deli sandwiches, she told Yancey how she had moved to New York about a year earlier from Wilmington, Delaware, where she had taught school after graduation.

"What made you move to New York?" Yancey asked. She remembered Windsor had a set of lungs on her and used to lead most of the songs for the gospel choir. Yancey figured she had come to New York to pursue music and sought out Yancey for advice. Yancey was prepared to tell her to get rid of her dreads and about forty pounds when Windsor announced she had moved to New York to get married, but quickly realized she was about to make the biggest mistake of her life.

"So you're not getting married?"

"Not now and probably not ever," Windsor said.

"So, do you still sing?" Yancey asked.

"Oh sometimes, but mostly I just sing for the Lord in my church choir."

"What are you doing to make ends meet? New York is an expensive city."

"I teach at a wonderful alternative school in the Village, the Harvey Milk School, and I do some volunteer work."

"What part of town do you live in?"

"I live in the Bronx, in Riverdale, but I'm looking for something a little closer to my job. My ex-boyfriend was nice enough to let me keep the place we had picked out, but I can't afford it without working two or three jobs."

While Windsor asked Yancey questions about how exciting it was to be on Broadway and television, Yancey was thinking how harmless Windsor might be for a roommate, and how the rent could help with making ends meet when she was unemployed.

"I think I might be able to help you out," Yancey said.

"How?"

"I have servant's quarters in my house. You come by and see it," Yancey said as she pulled the check from the black leather binder and reached in her wallet for a credit card. She looked at the bill and saw it was under twenty dollars, so she put the card back and pulled out a twenty-dollar bill.

"Oh, I would love to see it," Windsor said.

"How much are you paying for rent right now?" Yancey asked.

"Fifteen hundred."

"Well, if you like it, I could let you have it for a thousand," Yancey said.

"That sounds great. When can I come by?"

"Tomorrow. But in the afternoon. I'm a late sleeper,"

Yancey said. She wrote her address on the back of the bill.

"I'll come by after work."

"Great."

Windsor moved in a week later.

3

YANCEY WAS jolted awake by the sound of Basil's voice whispering, "Wake up, baby. I've got a surprise for you."

"What?" Yancey asked in a sleep-thickened voice. She rubbed her eyes and focused them on Basil, who was already dressed. It was the morning after Yancey's final performance in *Fosse,* which had been followed by a festive party with several cast members and too much wine. Basil knew Yancey would sometimes go through a mild depression after a job ended, especially when she didn't have something else lined up, so he decided to arrange a day of her favorite things.

"I have a surprise for you, but first I need to put this on you," Basil said as he revealed a black satin scarf.

"What are you up to? It's not my birthday." Yancey giggled.

"Just trust me," he said, gently wrapping the scarf

around Yancey's eyes. He then stood up and took Yancey's hands and led her into the dining room of his large loft. She was wearing one of Basil's silk T-shirts sans bra and a pair of his white cotton boxers. Yancey could hear soft jazz music playing and smelled the aroma of breakfast food.

"Are you ready for your surprise?" Basil whispered and kissed the back of her neck.

"Yes."

Basil removed the scarf from Yancey's eyes and she was greeted by a dining room filled with pink tulips and a table covered with red rose petals and china service for two. Shafts of the morning sun were filling the apartment with warm light. A handsome Hispanic man dressed in a black tuxedo and looking like the headwaiter in a five-star restaurant welcomed her. "Good morning, Ms. Braxton, welcome to a day designed especially for you." He had a white linen napkin draped over his left arm and with his free right hand he then pulled back the chair and motioned for Yancey to take her seat. Yancey smiled and nodded toward him, then looked at Basil. His smiling face glowed with pleasure. Basil's eyes widened when he saw the smile on Yancey's face, which was both seductive and sincere, her eyes filling with tears. She picked up the linen napkin and dabbed her eyes, then noticed a small plate filled with sections of tangerines, kiwis, and pink grapefruit drizzled in champagne. Basil had hired a small catering service his firm often used to prepare a brunch of fruit, eggs, waffles, and an array of breakfast meats for Yancey and himself. A florist had been commissioned to decorate the apartment in the flowers Yancey loved.

"Why did you do this?"

"Because I love you," Basil said.

"What did I do to deserve all this love?" Yancey asked.

"You were born," Basil replied quickly. At that moment Basil's heart was filled with so much love for Yancey he thought it would push right through his light-green cotton stretch sweater.

"Stop saying stuff like that! You're going to make me start bawling," Yancey said.

"You know I don't want to make you cry, it's just a special way to celebrate your new job," Basil said.

"But I don't have a new job. Don't you remember? Last night was the end. I'm unemployed. Again," Yancey said as she started to frown. The waiter moved close to Yancey and asked, "Can I offer you a mimosa or some coffee?"

"Let me have both," Yancey said, gazing at Basil with a quizzical look on her face, without even looking at the waiter.

"I know that look," he said. "You're wondering why I went through all this effort."

Yancey nodded her head and waited for his explanation.

"I just want you to know that I not only love you but I appreciate your talent as well. I don't want you to spend today or any other day wondering when the next job will come along."

"I love you," Yancey said, cherishing Basil's every word.

"And I love you more. Now eat up. I have a whole day planned."

"Tell me," Yancey demanded with an eager smile. She

raised her fork daintily and took a small portion of the eggs.

"As soon as we finish breakfast, I'm going to draw you a bath. And guess what?"

"What?"

"I'm going to bathe you with my clothes on. I don't want you to think about hittin' the skins," Basil answered gently.

"Then it's not going to be the bath I have in mind," Yancey said.

"Next we are going to the gym and work out. After that, I think we should stop by this store I know you love on Fifty-seventh and Fifth Avenue and see if they have something for my special lady."

Yancey clapped her hands in delight and asked, "Please tell me you're talking about Tiffany's?"

"If it's on Fifty-seventh and Fifth. Then we'll come back here for a candlelit dinner and I've bought DVD's of a couple of your favorite movies, including your all-time favorite, *All About Eve*."

"Stop it. I can't stand any more. Let's just finish breakfast so we can get started."

"Whatever you say, baby. This day is all about you."

YANCEY almost dropped the crystal salad bowl when I asked her a question at the end of her day. It was hard to believe after two years and the countless conversations we had had about our families that it had never come up. The question just sorta popped out of my mouth as I watched her rinse and pull apart the lettuce while we

prepared my favorite meal of salad, steak, and baked potatoes. In her black tight-fitting pants, and cashmere V-
neck sweater, Yancey looked like the most glamorous
housewife on earth, particularly since she was wearing
her Tiffany gift, dangling diamond earrings the size of
hazelnuts.

"How many children do I want?" she asked.

"Yeah, how many children do you want?" I repeated.

"Well, how many do you want?"

"I asked first," I teased.

Yancey placed the bowl filled with lettuce, cucumbers,
and tomatoes on the counter and walked over to where I
was leaning against the refrigerator. She stood between
my legs and placed her long, elegant arms on my shoulders and quizzed, "What brought this on?"

"You *do* want to have children, don't you?"

"Of course I do," she said, telling a little white lie. "But
I also want my career and I have to be married first," she
said firmly.

"But of course," I replied.

"I want a family one day also, but not one like mine,"
Yancey said.

"Me neither," I assured Yancey.

"I don't think you can call what you and I had a family,"
Yancey added.

"We'll create our own special family," I said. I kissed
her gently on the lips and then her forehead.

She kissed me back and said, "And only when we're
both ready."

• • •

I couldn't sleep that night. I kept thinking about children while stroking Yancey's face as she slept. The children Yancey and I would have. I knew they would be beautiful. I mean with Yancey's beautiful face, my gray eyes, our children would be the envy of any parents. When I think about having a family, I realize how I want it to be different from my childhood, and I know Yancey feels the same way. We both had f'd-up childhoods. I want my kids to wake up every morning knowing that both of their parents will be there to greet them. The same thing at night and at any activity they participate in. I could picture having a little boy who had mad football skills like his bad-assed dad.

I hoped that one day I would be selected for the Pro Football Hall of Fame. The other day I realized that I will be eligible in a couple of years. When I dream about being inducted, I always imagine a wife and a couple of kids right there in the front row. Maybe I could have my son introduce me, like Walter Payton's son did. When I saw Walter's young son, Jarrett, introduce his father, well, it almost brought me to tears. And for a man who never cries, that's a hard thing to do.

I know if I'm going to start a family then it means marriage. I'm pretty sure I'm ready. My finances are in order and I love Yancey more and more each day. I know her career is important, but I think she would give up just a little something to marry me and have my children—make that *our* children. The only question that lingers in my mind is can a diva and a dude like me ever settle down?

4

I THINK IT would be a waste of time for you to read for this part," the unsmiling casting agent said to a stunned Yancey.

"Why do you say that? I'd be perfect for the part," Yancey said. She was sitting on the edge of a leather swivel chair in a large and modern conference room in midtown Manhattan.

The dark-skinned, small-boned, and wiry lady with full, plum-colored lips picked up Yancey's head shot which was sitting on top of a stack of other pictures and said, "You're much darker in person than in this picture. The role calls for a mixed-race black woman."

The part was the lead role in an upcoming miniseries on the life of Sally Hemings, the alleged slave lover of President Thomas Jefferson. Yancey had heard about the audition not from her agent Lois but while eavesdropping on a backstage conversation between a couple of light-skinned beauties during an audition for a Broadway work-shop. Yancey thought even though it was television, this was a role she needed on her résumé, so she wasn't going to let the casting agent get in her way. She was also think-ing of the fifteen percent she could save with no greedy agent holding out her hands. So Yancey began to release a waterfall of charm, which she could turn off and on like a shower.

"I heard you're one of the top African American casting agents in the country. I love to see smart sisters taking control in this business," Yancey said. The woman didn't respond while she studied Yancey's picture, turning it over to review her résumé. Yancey was thinking how much she hated when black folks in charge acted so con-descending and arrogant. She also assumed the casting agent was envious of every light-skinned woman she had come across. Especially the beautiful ones. Over a year ago, Yancey had turned down an audition for a film for two reasons. One, her agent said it was an ensemble piece, and two, the casting agent was an African Ameri-can female. The film, *The Best Man,* written and directed by Malcom Lee, had become one of the year's biggest hits. Yancey remembered how she seethed while sitting through the film and would have walked out had Basil not been enjoying it so much. In fact, he had seen the film three times. Twice alone. Yet all Yancey felt while she watched the film was the sting of jealousy every time the strikingly beautiful Nia Long, with high cheekbones and the perfect short hairstyle, graced the screen. *I should be playing that role,* Yancey told herself over and over.

"Where did you hear that from?" the casting agent

asked when she finally stopped looking at the head shot. Her voice was flat and emotionless.

"Around. You know how word gets around." Yancey smiled automatically.

"Truth be told, I'm one of the tops in the business. Period."

"I'm sure you are."

"I still don't think I'm going to let you read because I have about ten young ladies who we've already tested on screen."

"That's a lovely sweater you have on. Is it cashmere?" Yancey asked. She leaned closer, as if to admire the mustard-yellow turtleneck sweater.

"No, it's a blend. Now, Miss Braxton, back to the role."

"You can call me Yancey."

"Yancey. I'm sure you're a talented young lady, but like I said, you're not the type. Sally Hemings was of mixed race."

"My father was white," Yancey lied.

"He was?" she asked with raised eyebrows.

"Yes."

"I can put you in contact with the agent handling the extra casting."

"I'm not interested in extra work," Yancey said firmly. She wanted to take off one of her suede backless pumps and throw it at the lady, who had a self-satisfied look every time she gave Yancey a reason why she wasn't right for the role. But Yancey reminded herself that she could get more with honey than with vinegar, so she offered a compromise after the agent mentioned her tight schedule.

"Who's the executive producer?" Yancey asked.

"Why?"

"I was thinking maybe I could do a test with him while you see the other girls."

"It's being produced by CBS, and seeing the executive producer on your own is not an option. I'll keep your head shot and résumé on file. You never know when I might be casting something you're right for," she said as she stood with an icy glare and extended her hand to Yancey. Realizing the meeting was over, Yancey tried to stop herself but couldn't and said, "You people like playing God, don't you?" and stormed out of the room.

5

I HAD JUST gotten home from dinner at Lola's on West Twenty-second with a hard-drinking client when the phone rang. I was hoping it was Yancey calling to give me the word to come over for a late-night bath. It wasn't.

"Dude! Where have you been?" a somewhat soft, trying-to-be-hard male voice said.

"Who is this?" I asked.

"This is Bradford. Remember, we met a couple of years ago at the gym on Sixty-sixth?"

I vaguely recalled this caramel-colored dancer with a real tight body who gave killer head. Bradford could deep-throat the jimmie like a fire-eating circus performer. We had hooked up a couple of times before I met Yancey and right after I gave up on Raymond.

"Oh yeah, whassup? I haven't heard from you in a while," I said.

"I know. I was doing a show over in London for a couple of years. I just got back in town a couple of days ago and you and that big ole dick of yours came across my mind," he said.

I was thinking I should have gotten all my numbers changed after I met Yancey, but I said, "Yo, dude, I hate to disappoint you and that magic tongue of yours, but I don't roll like that no more."

"What?"

"Yeah, I met a young lady and I'm keeping things real."

"I got the impression you liked what I could do. I'm not looking for romance. You don't even have to look at me. Just close your eyes and imagine my sweet lips are those of your lady. I know she probably don't get down like that. Before you open your eyes I will be gone and you can go to sleep with a smile on your face," Bradford promised.

For a moment I started thinking about Bradford's perfect bow lips, and as it had been a no-draws day I could feel my jimmie make his presence known by standing at attention and pressing against my suit pants at the mere memory of Bradford's last visit. I started to think maybe it wouldn't be so bad to give Bradford a go, and since Yancey was probably asleep, it would be kind of a no harm, no foul situation. So I was a little bit surprised at myself when I said, "You can't even compete with my lady, so I think I'm gonna have to pass. Welcome back home," I said and hung up the phone.

I stood silently for a minute and unbuckled my pants and let them drop, my jimmie not waving freely, but more like half-mast. I thought about getting it at full attention and then calling Yancey, but my thoughts went back to the phone call. Years ago, I wouldn't have been so polite with Bradford. When men were forward with me, it pissed me the fuck off. Still does. Sometimes I call them all kinda faggots, sissies, and other times I just let it pass. Damn, I hope I'm not becoming one of those good guys like Raymond.

6

YANCEY WAS standing silently in her dance studio, the nearly empty room where Yancey would often read scripts out loud and sometimes would do full song-and-dance routines in front of a mirrored wall that made the space seem almost as large as a rehearsal hall.

She was wearing a black leotard with a beige wrap-around short skirt and toe shoes. While Yancey was trying to decide if she wanted to dance or look at some of the television scripts Lois had messengered over, the telephone rang. Yancey ignored the ring and went into the kitchen to grab a bottle of water. She had drunk almost half of the bottle when the phone rang again. Again, she didn't answer it. After finishing the water, Yancey decided she felt like dancing and went to the bedroom to get a classical dance CD. Just as she pulled the CD from the wall unit, the phone rang again. Yancey looked at the answering machine and saw that whoever had called before didn't leave a message, so she decided to answer. *Maybe it's Lois with some big news she doesn't want to leave on the machine,* Yancey thought.

The minute Yancey picked up the receiver and heard the voice on the other end, she sighed deeply.

"Ms. Yancey Braxton, please."

"Speaking," Yancey said as she sat down on the bed.

"This is Mimi Evans from Diners Club," she said in the urgent voice all bill collectors possessed.

"What can I do for you?"

"Ms. Braxton, we just got a $9,800.00 charge resubmitted by a merchant. It seems we gave you a credit last month because we were told the item had been returned."

"What store?" Yancey asked even though she knew exactly who the merchant was. It was D'Anita, an exclusive dress shop on the Upper East Side. Yancey had purchased a beautiful evening gown when she decided to crash a record company party in the hope of slipping her demo tape to Sylvia Rhone of Elektra Records. The form-fitting sheer black gown with tiny diamonds around the neck and sleeves and a thigh-high split had been a hit with several men attending the party, but it didn't get her closer than a hundred feet to the CEO of one of the country's top labels. Yancey had only planned to stay about thirty minutes, come back home, get out of the gown, and return it the next day. She ended up staying three hours, and leaving the price tags on the dress couldn't disguise the fact the gown had been worn in a smoke-filled room.

"The store was D'Anita in New York City."

"I had my assistant take it back," Yancey declared. She had asked Windsor to drop the dress off, which she did. But a couple of hours later, the dress was returned to Yancey by messenger with a note saying the dress was soiled under the arms and could not be returned. The gown was still in the garment bag hanging in her closet.

"We talked to the merchant, and they told us it was returned after it had been worn."

"I never wore that dress. Besides, I thought you guys had some type of buyer's protection plan where you would take my side in a matter like this," Yancey said.

"We do, but just looking at the data I have here, I don't think we can help you, Ms. Braxton. So we have to request your payment in full immediately."

This is what Yancey hated about credit card companies like American Express and Diners Club. They gave you sky-high credit limits but expected their money every month. She had long maxed out the three Visas she had, so Diners Club was the last card she could use. She knew she had to pay the bill, even though she didn't have the money.

"I'll send you a check today," Yancey said. She was thinking about sending an unsigned check, which would give her a couple more weeks to get the money, but remembered she'd pulled that trick a few months prior.

"Will you be sending the full amount?"

"What do you mean?"

"Well, this month's balance is also due. With the $9,800.00 return and an additional $5,559.67 in new charges . . ." She paused for a second and Yancey figured she was adding the two numbers so she said, "You don't have to tell me the total amount. I can add."

"Is there any way you can send the payment with one of the overnight delivery services? Your account is in jeopardy of being sixty days past due. In that case your account would be subject to review, and we might have to pull a current credit report."

The mention of her credit report made Yancey's body warm. "No, I can't send it overnight! I'll send it via U.S. mail the way I always do. If that doesn't work then that's too damn tough," Yancey said. She slammed down the phone and began thinking about who she was going to call—Ava or Basil?

DAMN, girl, you look good," Basil said in a seductive murmur when Yancey walked into his bedroom wearing nothing but some red caviar–beaded ankle-strap pumps. Basil was already under the covers wearing nothing but a smile. They'd just returned from the opening night performance and party for the Dance Theater of Harlem, and watching the taut bodies of the dancers had set their hormones in full gallop. Not that Basil and Yancey needed human stimulants to aid their very active sex life. Basil was a supreme lover who had taken time to take her places no man had gone before. Basil loved the fact that Yancey could perform with the sexual confidence of rap star Li'l Kim and carry herself with the regal beauty of Halle Berry the moment her feet reached the floor.

The clear and melodious voice of Brian McKnight, one

of their favorite singers, was spilling into the room from the strategically placed speakers. They shared a small snifter of cognac and then made love for hours, caressing and kissing until a stillness fell over them and the room. Basil was enjoying the smell of Yancey's body mixed with the lingering trace of perfume, and Yancey loved the tenderness he showed after making love.

When Basil thought Yancey was asleep he gently moved her head from his chest and went into the kitchen to refill the snifter. He was surprised when he walked back into the bedroom and saw Yancey wide awake with a worried look on her face.

"What's the matter, baby? Was I gone too long? I thought you were getting some sleep." He sat on the edge of the bed.

"I've got a little problem." Her voice trembled and Yancey's eyes teared as she lowered her diamond-shaped face.

Basil lifted her tearstained face and said, "Tell me what's bothering you."

"I got a call today," Yancey said. Her voice sounded as soft as sand.

"From who?"

"From my bank. Some money I was expecting didn't come through yet and I've been writing checks, paying bills. I called my accountant and he told me a new system had been installed and payments were going to be late. My bank is threatening to close my account and I've got to have a checking account."

"Is that all? How much do you need?"

Yancey looked at Basil with a shocked look on her face and whispered, "Fifteen thousand."

"I'll have my accountant wire the money into your account tomorrow. You can pay me back when you get your money."

"Oh, baby . . . thank you," Yancey said, blushing with gratitude.

"No problem. Now you get some sleep. I'm going to take a shower."

Before he stood up, Yancey pulled Basil toward her and gave him a deep kiss as her fingertips explored the delicate details of the top of his sex. When Basil stood up his thick and round penis hung perfectly still. Yancey's face glowed with pleasure as her eyes passed over the backside of Basil's body like a laser as he walked into the bathroom. He loved when Yancey watched him walking around in the nude.

When he shut the door Yancey waited until she heard the rush of the shower and quickly picked up the phone and called Ava.

"Hello."

"Ava," Yancey whispered.

"Yes. Where are you?"

"I'm at Basil's."

"Why are you whispering?"

"I don't have long to talk. Basil's in the shower. I need to ask you a favor."

Without missing a beat Ava asked, "How much?"

"Fifteen thousand."

"How much?"

"Fifteen thousand. I need to pay for a dress they wouldn't let me return. You remember the dress I wore trying to get my demo to Sylvia Rhone?"

"Honey, you must think rich husbands grow on trees. I haven't gotten this one trained yet the way I like. We still have separate accounts. Besides, you're a big enough star where you should be getting your dresses and jewelry for free. You need a publicist or a manager to make that happen. I know this wonderful designer down in Dallas who is just fabulous. His name is Mark Anthony Hankins. I need to call him and see if we can't get you a couple of free dresses," Ava said.

Yancey took a deep breath. She needed money, not another lecture. So she said the words she knew Ava wanted to hear, "You're absolutely right. Can you talk to him for me?"

"Sure I will. I buy at least six gowns a year from him."

"So will you loan me the money?"

"Loan? I know I'm not getting this money back, Yancey, you need to stop wasting time with that ex-jock and get you a rich man. There are lots of Internet geeks out there who would love to marry somebody as beautiful as you. They might not be able to make love like Basil, but there ain't nothing that says you can't have someone like Basil on the side."

"Ava, please. There's a phone in the bathroom."

"Honey, men have somebody on the side all the time. I'll send you a check tomorrow."

"Can you wire it?"

"I could but I'd rather send it overnight express," Ava said, laughing to herself.

"What are you laughing about?" Yancey asked.

"There is this handsome Hispanic guy who picks up and delivers in my neighborhood. He's fine and I've been flirting with him. Wearing a little less each time he rings my bell. So let me send it through him."

"You better be careful."

"I am always careful, but I got to see if I can still work the young guys," Ava said.

"Okay, send it that way, but please do it tomorrow."

"I will."

"Thanks, Ava. I've got to go, I just heard the shower stop."

Yancey hung up the phone and readied herself to sleep soundly and peacefully in Basil's arms.

7

I WAS IN a deep sleep when my phone's second line startled me. In the B.Y. (Before Yancey) days I used to call it my hot line. And it was. A private telephone line just for the freaks like my boy Bradford. Booty Call Central. If I wasn't in the mood for something low-down and nasty, I'd just let the phone ring. Now when the line rings I know it's one of my clients or my seven-year-old nephew, Cade. I gave him the number because he's already telling me when he goes pro, I'm going to be his agent. Cade only calls after school and on Saturday mornings to remind me to watch *The X-Men,* so when the hot line rang at 2:30 A.M., I figured trouble had to be calling.

"Yeah," I grumbled after I picked up the phone.

"You have a collect call from a Cavell Clemmons. The call is coming from a correctional institution," the female voice said.

I immediately sat up in my bed and turned on the

lamp next to my phone and said, "Yes, I'll accept the call."
A few seconds later I heard Cavell's stressful voice.

"Thanks for taking my call, Basil. Man, I'm in deep trouble."

"Whassup, dude? Where are you?"

"I'm in jail, Basil. My wife had me arrested," Cavell said.

Cavell Clemmons was a former client and someone who I thought had everything on the ball. He had played for more than four years for the New Jersey Warriors as running back. Three of those years he was All Pro, but after a series of injuries, the Warriors cut Cavell and he really hadn't been the same since.

"What happened?"

"It's a long story, but what I need right now is for you to bail me out. I'm good for it, Basil. I got some money coming from a football camp I did. I just got to get out of here before my kids get up in the morning."

"Cavell, where am I going to get bail money this time of night? I don't keep a truckload of money here at the house. I'll do it first thing in the morning. But you need to tell me why your wife had you arrested," I said.

"I got caught cheatin'," Cavell said. His voice sounded like a little boy who had just got caught stealing money from his mother's purse.

"I know they didn't pick you up for cheating. Shit, if that was the case they couldn't build enough jails," I joked, trying to lighten up the phone call. Cavell didn't laugh.

"Man, the bitch installed some kind of spy phones in our house and was recording all my conversations with the freak I been fucking for the last six months. I mean, for months she's been dropping hints about knowing more than I thought she knew. She asked me flat out if I was cheating and I said no. That's when she hit the remote control and all over my house I hear me and the chick talking nasty and making plans. I was mad as fuck and I just lost my temper and slapped her a couple of times. She called 911 and the next thing I know the police are busting into my house."

"This sounds like some shit from a soap opera. Man, where are women learning this kinda shit? Fucking spy phones."

"Probably from watching soap operas or some damn talk show."

"You didn't hurt her badly, did you?"

"Man, I don't know. All I know is that I got busted and it just made me snap. She's talking about taking my kids and moving back to Macon. Said she was gonna git what little money I have left."

"Do you have a lawyer?"

"Not one for shit like this."

"Give me the information and I'll try and get down there first thing in the morning," I said.

While Cavell gave me the location of the jail, I couldn't help but think how much his life had changed since he had been cut from the league. I had seen cases like this more times than I wanted to remember. When I first signed Cavell out of the University of Georgia he seemed to be the model citizen. Almost every time I talked to him it was "Praise the Lord" this and "Praise the Lord" that. He even graduated on time with a degree in sports management. But no sooner than he made his first Pro Bowl he became a card carrying member of the "Dick in one hand, Bible in the other" bunch. Bible study on Wednesday night, tittie bar on Thursday. Since he left the NFL he had a lot of jobs coaching at kiddie football camps. I almost suggested the agency hire him as a scout or a full-fledged agent. I was suddenly happy it had remained just a thought.

"Basil, I appreciate this, man. I promise to git the money right back."

"Alright, dude, just try and get some sleep."

"It's obvious you ain't never been in the joint, dude. I don't plan to shut my eyes tonight. There's some big mutherfuckers in here and the guard told me they don't take too kindly to woman beaters and child molesters."

Imagine that, I thought as I hung up the phone and turned out the lamp.

8

YANCEY SLUNG her black leather bag on the sofa, picked up the phone, and dialed the number for Basil's office. When his assistant came on the phone Yancey said, "I need to speak with Mr. Henderson immediately."

"I think he's on the phone with his sister. Can I have him call you back?" she asked.

"Did you hear me? I need to speak with him now! Tell him it's important."

A couple of minutes later, Basil came on the line. "Baby, why you giving my assistant such a hard time? Didn't she tell you I'd call you back?"

"I need to talk to you now," Yancey said in a high-pitched voice. He could tell she was near tears.

"Are you alright? I mean, physically?"

"What do you mean by that? Of course I'm fine physically, but I need to talk to you right now."

"You said that. But if you're not in any kind of physical danger, then I need to get back to my call."

"Who are you talking to?" Yancey demanded.

"I was talking to Campbell about spending some time with Cade. What's the matter with you?"

"You're not listening to me. I said I need to talk to you. A casting agent actually had the nerve to dismiss me today without even having me read or dance!" Yancey said.

"Is that what you're so upset about? Baby, you'll get another job soon."

"Don't you care how I feel? I thought you understood what it's like out there for me. You said you'd always be there for me!" Yancey screamed.

"And I will be, but I've got to take care of my family as well. Let me call you back or, better yet, I'll come and take you to dinner after I stop by and see Cade," Basil offered.

"If you can't talk to me now, then forget it. I don't need your pity. Go spend time with your little nephew!" Yancey said and slammed down the phone.

Yancey was heading toward her bedroom to wait for Basil to call back and say he was sorry when Windsor walked out of the kitchen with a dishcloth in one hand and a large spoon in the other. Windsor was wearing a pale-blue shapeless dress that looked like something Yancey's grandmother used to wear to PTA meetings. She had gold hoops dangling from her ears. She heard Yancey screaming into the phone and knew there was diva turbulence in the area.

"You alright, Yancey?" she asked.

"I'm fine," Yancey said as she reached for her bag.

"Are you hungry? I cooked."

Yancey started to say, "What else is new?" It seemed as though every evening when Windsor wasn't working she was cooking. But Yancey was hungry and mad. "What did you make?" she asked.

"Come on into the kitchen and smell," Windsor said, motioning toward the kitchen with the dishcloth.

Yancey walked into the kitchen and was greeted by air thick with the smell of fried meat. Windsor had cooked fried chicken, rice and gravy, string beans, and homemade rolls.

"Let me fix you a plate and you tell me what's the matter."

Yancey took a seat at the granite kitchen counter and told her roommate how she had gone to audition for a new musical by George Wolfe. She told Windsor how it was going to be the hottest musical of the season and suddenly the female lead had left the workshop to get married. Windsor listened intently as she poured a cup of sugar into a pitcher of freshly squeezed lemons and water.

"This is going to be a great role and it's not going to Audra or Vanessa," Yancey said before taking a sip of the lemonade Windsor had placed in front of her.

"How do you know you didn't get the part?" Windsor asked as she piled a couple of pieces of golden-brown chicken on a cobalt-blue plate and pulled out a yellow linen napkin from a nearby drawer.

"Right after I sang my song I knew I wouldn't get this job. I sang my standard audition number. A song from a show I saw in Nashville once. The show was *Merrily We Roll Along* and the song is called 'Not a Day Goes By.' It's a beautiful song by Stephen Sondheim, and I was in perfect voice. My agent had told me to prepare two songs to sing. But right after I finished the first, the casting agent just said, 'Thank you.' Now I know you don't know much about the theater, but that is the kiss of death. It's like saying, 'Kiss my ass, bitch. You have no talent.'"

"Now, Yancey, you know that's not true. You're one of the most talented people I've ever seen on stage. And look how beautiful you look today."

Yancey was getting ready to bite into a piece of the chicken when Windsor quickly grabbed her hand and said, "Let's say grace."

Yancey looked at her as if she were crazy and said, "You go ahead."

Windsor closed her eyes and looked toward the ceiling and started to pray. "Lord, we thank you for this food our bodies are about to receive. We thank you for this day and the blessing of life. Lord, we ask that you help Yancey to understand that something good will come from disappointment. That you're a good God and you know what's best for us. Lord, most of all we just thank you for being you and loving us and dying for our sins. Amen."

When Windsor opened her eyes Yancey was staring at her in amazement. "Girl, you sound like a preacher."

Windsor ignored Yancey's comment and asked, "Is that what you wore to the audition?"

"Yes," Yancey said. She took a bit of the piping-hot chicken. Windsor looked at her in amazement, since she had never seen Yancey take a bite of anything that remotely looked like it had been drenched in hot oil. Yancey was wearing a pale pink, tight silk skirt with a black short-sleeved cashmere sweater complemented by a thin string of pearls around her neck. Her hair was pulled back, revealing matching pearl earrings. While Yancey was eating, Windsor unloaded an arsenal of supportive words. "You will be just fine. That casting person is going to wake up tonight and say, 'What am I doing? I just turned down the most talented and beautiful woman in New York City.' Trust me, you'll be getting a call very soon and if not for that job, then something much, much better."

"Can you cast a spell on him?" Yancey joked.

"Now, Yancey, you know I don't believe in any of that demonic stuff. You just put it in the hands of the Lord," Windsor said.

"So you think that's better than a spell or just finding out who got the job and kicking her ass?" Yancey quizzed.

"I know it is," Windsor said confidently.

"So what do you have planned for this evening?"

"I rented a movie. You want to watch it with me?" Windsor asked.

"What did you get?"

"*A Perfect Murder.*"

"I've already seen that, I think. Isn't that with Michael Douglas and Gwyneth Paltrow?"

"I think so."

"Yeah, I saw that. It's pretty good, and nobody plays 'white girl' like Gwyneth Paltrow," Yancey said before she took a final bite of the chicken.

After Yancey had devoured the entire plate of food, she looked at Windsor and said, "I'm so emotionally spent. Can you run me a hot bath?"

"Sure. I'll do that for you. So, did you enjoy dinner?"

Windsor asked. She took the black skillet filled with grease over to the sink and poured it out.

"It was alright. But I can't eat like that every day. If I did, I'd need more than the Lord to help my career. I'd be big as some of them mamas always singing background," Yancey said as she dabbed her lips with the napkin and dropped it on the clean plate.

"How did you lose the weight?" Windsor asked.

"What are you talking about?" Yancey asked.

"Oh, I saw you once leaving the HU clinic, and between me and you, it looked like you had gained a little weight since I first met you. I mean, we used to talk about what a wonderful shape you had when you moved into the dorm. We hated you," Windsor laughed.

"Trust me when I say this . . . I have *never* been overweight and I never will be," Yancey said. She got up from the bar stool and headed toward her bedroom.

9

I WON!" CAMPBELL screamed, clapping her hands and raising her arms in the air victoriously.

"I think you cheated," I said.

"I don't need to cheat, big brother."

"I just let you win," I teased after I had lost another game of Scrabble to my sister.

I had decided to spend the evening in her Brooklyn apartment, since I knew soon I was going to be out on the road a lot courting football players after practice and games. Campbell had cooked a wonderful dinner of red snapper topped with scalloped potatoes with some creamed spinach on the side. Cade wanted chicken fingers, but I convinced him fish and spinach were good for building muscles.

I tried to spend at least one evening a week with my sister and her family. It was a time when I could let my guard down. I didn't have to worry about what mofos or Yancey were thinking.

We took turns on where we would gather. Sometimes I would invite them to my loft and would order pizza, or sometimes I would break down and cook a real meal myself. I can do a thing or two with my George Foreman grill. We always played Scrabble or cards after dinner, especially when Hewitt and Yancey joined us. Hewitt's job as an inspector for U.S. Airways kept him on the road, and Yancey was always doing some show. When Campbell's job selling real estate in the Mount Vernon and White Plains area caused her to run late, I would pick Cade up from school and the two of us would hang out until Campbell would call me on my celly.

"So how long are you going to be out of town?" Campbell asked.

"This time of year is when I really have to work. Starting in September until December I can count on spending at least four nights a week on the road in places like Fayetteville, Arkansas, Tallahassee, Florida, and College Station, Texas," I said.

"I know that doesn't sit too well with Yancey," Campbell said.

"No, it doesn't. Right now she's not too happy with me 'cause some audition didn't go well, and she wanted me to make her feel better. I told her I was going to see Cade."

"Trust me, I understand her. Hewitt has been traveling a lot lately. Right now he's up in Albany for a couple of days," Campbell said.

"So you siding with Yancey? You supposed to have my back, sister. Besides, sometimes Yancey needs to realize she's not the only star in my show."

"I'm sure she don't want to hear that, and you know I got your back." She smiled.

I looked at my watch and realized it was a little past nine and time for me to head back to Manhattan and pack for my trip. But I couldn't do that without saying good night to my favorite little man, so I called his name, and out he came running like an All-American running back.

"Cade! Stop running," Campbell said. "Your uncle is getting ready to leave. Give him a hug." He was wearing his New York Yankee pajamas and he still had on his socks.

"Cade, did you tell your uncle what you're wearing for Halloween?"

Cade smiled and shook his head and said, "Naw." I looked at Campbell and then at Cade and asked, "What? Stone Cold Steve Austin?"

"It's a surprise," Cade said.

"It's okay. You can tell him since it's only a couple weeks away and Uncle Basil might not be in town. He has to go out of town for work."

Cade jumped up and down, pointed at me, and said, "I'm going as you. I'm going to be a New Jersey Warrior." I couldn't do anything but smile as I again looked at Cade and then Campbell.

"We found a place on the Internet where we can buy a kid's uniform with your number on it," Campbell said. Cade had a pleased smile on his face.

"If I'm out of town, will you take pictures for me, Cade?"

"Yep!"

"You gonna miss me while I'm gone?" I asked Cade.

"I want to go with you," Cade said, his face full of a child's tenderness and vulnerability.

"I wish I could take you with me, but you've got school."

"Mommy could write me a note and say I was helping you with your work," he said.

"But who's gonna stay here with me?" Campbell asked.

"Daddy will be back soon," he replied.

I bent down so that I was at eye level with Cade, whose gray eyes were almost identical to my own. "You know I wish I could take you with me, but you got to be the man and stay here and take care of Mommy, okay?" I palmed his head playfully.

"Okay," he said with the mournful face he often used to get his way.

"Give me a hug," I said, and we squeezed each other tightly for over a minute. As I held him, I was thinking how much I loved this little boy and of the day when I would have children of my own. I almost lost it when Cade whispered, "I love you a whole lot, Uncle Basil." It didn't matter how many times I'd heard him say the words, they always touched my heart in a way it had never been touched.

I rubbed his head gently and said, "And I love you a whole lot too."

1 0

I<small>T WAS</small> Sunday evening. Windsor was at church and Yancey was snuggled up on her sofa eating fried rice with chopsticks, watching her favorite television show, *Sex and the City*. One moment she was laughing, and the next she thought, *These skinny white bitches need a black girlfriend.*

Yancey removed the sky-blue cashmere blanket covering her naked legs, put the rice and chopsticks on the coffee table, and picked up her cordless phone. After she had dialed the number, she put the sound on mute, then took a small sip of her now warm white wine.

"Drew residence," a young child answered.

"Is Lois in?" Yancey asked.

"You mean my mommy?"

"Yes, is she in? Tell her it's Yancey Braxton."

A few moments later Yancey heard her agent, Lois Drew, on the other line.

"Yancey, is everything alright?"

"Not really," Yancey said coolly. She knew Lois didn't like to be called at home and had only given her the number when Yancey made it a condition of doing business. Lois was her third agent in a year. Yancey had recently left the prestigious William Morris Agency after they signed Nicole Springer, a Broadway actress whom Yancey considered her archrival. Yancey despised Nicole so much that she had spiked her coffee with a laxative when the two were doing *Dreamgirls*. It was classic *All About Eve* drama. Yancey still had nightmares sometimes, in which Nicole slapped her in a theater full of people, right after she had beaten out Yancey for the Tony Award, while a beautiful little girl pointed and laughed at Yancey's crimson face.

"What's the matter? I was just getting ready to read my daughter a story before I put her to bed."

"I want to be on *Sex and the City*," Yancey said in a matter-of-fact voice.

"What? You want to be on who?"

Yancey pulled the phone from her ear and gave it a *what's wrong with this bitch* look, then put it back to her ear and said, "I want to be on *Sex and the City*. Can you believe that a show based in New York doesn't have some fabulous black diva having sex as well? We do have sex, you know."

"We've never had any requests from the producers fitting your profile, Yancey. I'm sure I can get you some extra work on the show, which, you know, could lead to speaking parts when they come up."

"Now, Lois, I can't be hearing you correctly. You know I don't do extra work."

"I know, Yancey. And it's not something I would even bring up. But sometimes you have to find another way to crack a nut." Lois was beginning to think she needed a chart to keep track of the things this particular client wouldn't do. No extra work, no soap operas, no shows where her name wasn't listed above the title, and so on and so on.

Again Yancey pulled the phone away from her ear and stared at it. When she placed it back on her ear, she raised the level of her voice and said, "Look, Lois, when I signed on with you and your agency, you promised to treat me like a major star. Now correct me if I'm wrong, but if one of your little blonde, blue-eyed no-talent clients called and asked you to get her a reading with a show, you wouldn't recommend that they pursue extra work, now, would you?"

Lois took a deep breath and said, "Yancey, we can't make this a racial thing. You know me better than that."

"All I know is I want to be on *Sex and the City,* and not as some damn extra. Now since you're my agent, it's your job to make it happen. When I was at William Morris, they never had a problem sending me on casting calls that didn't specify a beautiful African American woman. Call me when you've set up my audition. Good evening!" Yancey said. She pressed the "end" button on her phone.

ABOUT thirty minutes later, Yancey's phone rang. She thought maybe it was Lois trying to calm her down, but her caller ID displayed Basil's cellular number. Yancey smiled to herself, remembering the battle that ensued when she insisted that Basil remove the block on his home and cellular phone numbers. All it took was a couple of days of her not picking up the phone.

"Hey, baby," Yancey purred into the phone.

"Hey, yourself. So you're over your diva moment? Did you miss me?"

"Of course I missed you. Where are you?"

"At baggage claim waiting on my luggage. Just got back from Florida. Do you feel like some company?"

"That depends on who it is," Yancey teased.

"Me and my special friend." Basil laughed.

"Do I know him?"

"Oh, yeah, and he loves you."

"Then I guess I'll start a bath for the both of you," Yancey said.

"Where's your roomie?"

"Baby, it's Sunday and you know Sister Windsor is at church."

"Do you want to come over to my place instead?"

"You come on over here. We will be well into our bath before she comes in. Besides, I got something special to go with our bath. Should I get it ready?"

"You do that. By the way, I signed another for-sure first-round pick, and he's a white boy." Basil laughed.

"That's great! I have some big news too."

"What?" Basil asked.

"I should make you wait, but since you shared your big news with me, I'm going to be on *Sex and the City,*" Yancey said.

"Baby, that's one of your favorite shows. I'm so proud of you," Basil said.

"Then get your luggage and come over here and show me how proud you are," Yancey said as she glanced at her smiling reflection in the mirror.

ABOUT an hour later Yancey's doorbell rang. She looked at herself once again in the mirror, then looked out the peephole, from which she could scan his handsome profile and watch Basil adjust his tie. She ran to turn on the music she had placed in her CD system, then raced to open the door wearing nothing but a black sheer teddy that cupped the lines of her breasts and hips. Nina Simone's "I Could Put a Spell on You" was playing in the background.

"Girl . . . girl . . . girl. You make me want to make sweet, sweet love to you right here," Basil said as he grabbed Yancey and hugged her tightly. He moved into the townhouse, shut the door with his foot, then kissed Yancey as he dropped his garment bag on the floor. Her lips were soft and warm and he could taste the white wine on her breath.

"Did you miss me, girl?" Basil whispered.

"Let me show you how much I missed you," Yancey said. She pulled back from Basil and removed his jacket while he released his tie and started unbuttoning his shirt. Within a few seconds Basil was standing before her with an erection that brought to mind a foot-long hot dog. He took in a deep breath of Yancey's fresh-smelling hair, then settled his mouth in the bend of her neck. Right when Yancey thought she could stand no more, he let one of his hands drop to her opening. He gently inserted his beefy index finger into her and moved it around, caressing her insides and delighting himself in her moans of approval.

Basil picked up Yancey and carried her from the foyer to the bedroom. Once in the bedroom, he laid her gently on the bed. Starting at her head, he licked and massaged his way over all points of her beautiful body. He nestled his head between her legs, sucking and nibbling her to total ecstasy.

Making his way down Yancey's body as if it were a map, he opened his mouth and took in each of her toes one by one, savoring them as if each had been sprinkled with cinnamon sugar. Yancey was nearly spent and the real ride had not even begun.

Basil lifted Yancey and placed her on top of him. He entered her slowly, then pulled back before he thrust into her. Yancey rode his manhood like she was a rodeo queen defending her title. His whole body shook with passion. Basil was sweating like a cold beer on a hot summer day. They moved to a music that was all their own. Fast, slow, and then fast again, but in an orchestrated way that could only be played by two who knew each other very well. Their bodies communicated in a way that they both knew said they were making love like they meant it. As they whispered their own special dirty talk, their movements became even more intense until, in unison, they both let go, unable to resist the intense, sweet release.

Yancey and Basil were both exhausted and intoxicated

with pleasure. After a few minutes of labored breathing, Basil looked over at Yancey and said, "So, I guess you must have really missed me." Yancey just gave a sexy smile that let him know she was ready for the second act.

1 1

IT WAS Monday evening and Yancey had just walked in the door from a class at the Broadway Dance Center and was looking forward to spending the evening with Basil. When she had talked to him right before her dance lesson, Basil suggested he pick up some sushi and come over for a nice bottle of wine and a bath. Instead of Basil, Yancey was greeted by Windsor, whose eyes looked bright and urgent. Her face had only the faintest touch of makeup, and she was wearing a purple bandana as a headband.

"I'm so glad you're home," she said.

"Who were you expecting?" Yancey asked.

"Oh, I mean, I need to ask you a big, big favor," Windsor said.

"What?" Yancey asked. She dropped her dance bag on the floor at the edge of the sofa.

"Can you help me out at Hale House tonight?" Windsor asked. Hale House was an organization in Harlem that housed HIV and drug-addicted babies. Windsor gave her free time there a couple nights a week and also helped schedule other volunteers.

"You need a check or something? Sure, I can do that," Yancey said as she picked up the mail and looked through it. Realizing it was all bills, she placed them back on the sofa table.

"I'm not asking for a check, even though that would be wonderful. I need you to come up with me and hold the babies."

"Hold the babies? What are you talking about?"

"Two of my ladies are sick tonight, and I need someone to come up and just hold the babies. You don't have to read to them or anything. Just hold them. They love being held," Windsor said with a big warm smile.

"I wish I could, but I have a date this evening with Basil," Yancey said. She started toward the bar area for a bottle of sparkling water.

"No, you don't," Windsor said.

Yancey turned around and quizzed, "What did you say?"

"Basil called and said he was going to be real late because one of his clients came into town unexpectedly and he was taking him to dinner."

"I can't believe this shit! What were you doing answering my private line?" Yancey demanded.

"I didn't. He called me on my phone. He said he knew you were in class."

"Oh, did he?" Yancey asked curtly. She studied Windsor's face to try and determine if there was anything smug about the way she was looking at her. There was not. She could feel her own face begin to flush. She couldn't wait to tell Basil never to cancel their plans with her roommate. He was also due for another lecture on who was first in his life—Yancey, not the three Cs . . . Cade, Campbell, or Clients.

"So, will you help? I promise you won't regret it. The babies are all just so beautiful."

Yancey took a few steps and dropped herself on the couch and picked up the remote control before announcing, "I'm going to watch that millionaire show and I don't do babies. They don't like me and I don't like them!"

A surprised and disappointed Windsor turned and walked out the door.

THE next morning Windsor walked into the kitchen for a glass of juice. Yancey was leaning against the sink, fully made up with a satisfied smile on her face. She was drinking coffee from a black-and-yellow mug from the show *Cats*.

"Good morning. How are you doing?" Yancey asked.

"I'm blessed and highly favored," Windsor replied as she opened the refrigerator and pulled out a plastic jug of cranberry juice.

"I have something for you," Yancey said. She pulled an envelope out of her pocket and handed it to Windsor.

"What's this?"

"Open it and see."

Windsor tore open the light-pink envelope with Yancey's full name and address personalized in black script lettering. On the inside was a check made payable to Hale House in the amount of fifteen hundred dollars.

"Yancey, this is too much. Are you sure you want to do this?"

"Sure. I'm sorry about last night, and I just wanted to do something." Yancey smiled.

"We appreciate this, but I still think you ought to come and hold the babies."

Yancey poured herself another cup of coffee. Her back was to Windsor as she said softly, "I told you I'm not good with kids. Maybe the money will help for some baby holders."

"We don't pay the volunteers. Don't you plan to have children when you get married?"

"I'll deal with that road when I come to it. I don't even know if I'll ever get married. Right now all I want to do is concentrate on my career."

"We sure had you pegged wrong," Windsor said. She took a sip of her juice.

"What are you talking about?"

"Back at Howard. Some of the girls in the dorm just figured you'd be married with a lot of kids by now to that ROTC guy . . . What was his name?" Windsor asked.

"That was in the past, let's leave it there. Is that check enough?"

"It's wonderful, Yancey, thank you. I will drop this check off with Lorraine Hale right after I leave work today," Windsor said as she moved toward Yancey and covered her slender body with both of her large arms and whispered, "The babies thank you from the bottom of their little hearts."

1 2

WAS IN my office getting ready to call Yancey and apologize for breaking our date when my assistant, Kendra, buzzed me and told me she was on the line. I didn't know what to expect since she hadn't picked up her phone after I called her when I got home.

"Hey, baby. Did you miss me last night?" I said.

"Don't try and give me that baby stuff. I'm mad at you," Yancey said.

"But you still love me, right?"

"Only if you do something for me."

"What do you have in mind?" I said in my best Barry White voice.

"Windsor works with these kids at some place called Hale House, and she asked me for a contribution," Yancey said.

"I know about Hale House. I went to some big dinner

they gave a couple of years ago," I said. "They do great work."

"Yeah, that's what Windsor said. I gave her a check this morning 'cause I knew you would want to give."

"How much did I give?" I asked as I smiled to myself. I love the way Yancey was always concerned with others.

"Five thousand dollars," Yancey said.

"I'll give you a check when I see you later this evening."

"That's fine, and yes, I still love you," Yancey whispered.

I was getting ready to tell Yancey I loved her when I noticed Brison tapping at my door.

"I love you, baby, but I got to run," I said. I hung up the phone and motioned for Brison to enter my office.

"You got a minute?" he asked.

"Sure. Whassup?" Brison still looked as if he could line up on the defense for any NFL team. He was a beefy-faced man with large hands. He was just a little over six six, with toast-brown skin and a bald head. He was the married man in the office and had three children and a beautiful wife, Sherrie, who loved planning parties for the firm. Nico, his brother-in-law, was single. He traveled more than Brison and myself simply because he had ladies in almost every major city in the country. Whenever we had a player who could be easily influenced by a quick piece of ass, Nico knew some woman who was more than willing to fill the player's request. Brison didn't think it was the best way to conduct business, but sometimes a beautiful woman, with freak tendencies, could be the difference between a player signing with us or going with the competition. Nico and I hated to lose more than anything.

"When are you going back to the Chicago area?" Brison asked as he sat on my brown overstuffed sofa. My office was hooked up real nice. I had colorful artwork on the walls and a rich redwood conference table with black leather chairs. My desk was a large glasstop with solid brass legs. I also had a couple of antique end tables and lamps that created the feel of an upscale cigar bar.

"I don't know. I hadn't planned a trip there anytime soon," I said.

"Well, there's a guy there I want you to meet. I think he'd be a great candidate to bring into the firm, either as an employee to open the Chicago office or even as a partner, if he has the amount of money I think he has. He's a former teammate of mine from the Cougars. Plus he's really popular in Chicago," Brison said.

"Does he have any experience representing players?"

"Yeah, and that's one of the great things about him. He's with a white agency right now, but looking to leave. He already has two players from Northwestern and that guy Bennie Wilson from Michigan."

"Bennie Wilson! Man, he's certain to be a first-round pick."

"You know, dude, if we could get Bennie as a client we could end up with eight of the first ten picks," Brison said with a huge smile on his face. "That would drive the white boys wild."

"So you think right now is the time to expand?"

"I think so. When Nico gets back from his trip we should talk about it in more depth. But I think the Big

Ten area is too lucrative not to have some permanent representation there. I mean, Weinberg and company are
getting all the players from Michigan to Penn State. I
mean, they got those schools locked up tight. I think now
is the time to add some local color."

"I feel you," I said. I took a look at my desk calendar.
Nothing scheduled until late next week. "Look, Brison, I
can make a day trip to Chicago and meet with dude."

"You sure? I would do it, but I promised my son I
would coach his peewee team again. Next week is the
first practice."

"No problem. Just tell me where to go."

"I'll have Angela set everything up. I also got some
background information you can look over on the plane,"
Brison said.

"Cool. Who is the dude?"

"His name is Zurich Robinson."

13

YANCEY HAD just completed her weekly voice lesson and had stopped home to pick up her workout gear. She bounced into her house and was welcomed by a ringing phone. Yancey started to walk into the bedroom where the caller ID display was, but instead she lifted the receiver.

"Hello."

"Yancey?"

"Yes." The female voice sounded familiar, but Yancey wasn't certain.

"Please hold on for Lois," said Debbie, the personal assistant to Yancey's agent.

A few seconds later Lois came on the line. "I have wonderful news," Lois said.

"What? Did you get me an audition with *Sex and the City*?" She could tell Lois was excited about something and thought it had to be what Yancey wanted so badly.

"No, but I'm still working on that," Lois said.

"Then what? I hope you're not calling me for some local commercial or something."

"No, it's not a commercial. I just got a call from the producers of *Chicago* in Las Vegas, and they want you to take over the lead when Jasmine Guy leaves the show."

"What? I don't want to live in Las Vegas. Have you lost your mind?" Yancey screamed. "I want to be the first one in the lead! I don't want some role that everybody and their mama have played."

"Now wait, Yancey. I'm not finished. It's only for a month and they promise if you do this, you can either come back to Broadway or go to London. I think it's a great opportunity, because there is no end in sight for this show, and you don't even have to audition," Lois said.

"Audition? I know they aren't foolish enough to ask me to do anything but show up. I know that show like the back of my hand, but why do you think I should do this?"

"Because a lot of Hollywood heavyweights, meaning producers and directors, frequent Vegas all the time. I'll send out announcement cards and this could lead to some movie roles. You can get to L.A. in less than an hour by plane."

"I don't know. You know how much I love New York, and Basil is spending more time here. How much are they offering?"

"I think we're in a position to name our price," Lois said confidently.

"Tell them I want fifteen thousand and a percentage of the weekly gross," Yancey demanded.

"I don't know if I can do that, I mean the weekly gross

thing, but I'll get you the best deal possible. This could really be big, especially when you come back to New York."

"See what you can do." Yancey was always pushing Lois to be more aggressive. If she had the time, she'd be her own agent, manager, and publicist. No one could promote Yancey like Yancey.

"I'll call them back right now. How long are you going to be home?"

"I'm getting ready to run out."

"Can you give me thirty minutes?"

"I'll give you fifteen," Yancey said and hung up the phone.

A few minutes later the phone rang again while Yancey was preparing some tea. *Damn, that was fast,* she thought. When she picked up the phone, the last thing Yancey was expecting was a voice from her past.

"Is this Yancey Braxton?" a familiar female voice asked.

"This is Yancey. Who's calling?"

"This is Charlesetta Lewis. You don't remember my voice?"

"Mrs. Lewis. What a surprise. How are you doing? How's Derrick?" The question Yancey most wanted to ask the mother of her former longtime boyfriend was how she got Yancey's unlisted number.

"He's doing alright. I understand things are going really good for you with your showbiz stuff."

"Yes, I thought this was a call from my agent. My, it's been over five years since I heard from you," Yancey said as she took a seat in the chair next to her phone stand. She placed her free hand on the back of her neck and felt a thin film of perspiration. Her heart was beating at a swifter pace.

"Try six years," Mrs. Lewis said bluntly. There was no love lost between the two women.

"That long?" Yancey said, stifling a yawn.

"Yancey, I'm not going to beat around the bush. This isn't a social call, especially since you and me ain't never been that social."

"But you said Derrick was fine." Derrick Wayne Lewis was the man Yancey had fallen madly in love with during her first year at Howard University. They met when Yancey had nervously dropped her registration cards outside the Student Union. When she knelt down to pick them up, Derrick's strong hand extended the cards with a bright smile. It was a case of love at first touch. For two years it had been the perfect love affair. Yancey had wanted to get married. She was even willing to give up her career in beauty pageants and her dreams of Broadway to create the family she never had. For the very first time in her life Yancey felt *love*. Derrick loved Yancey, but he was in the ROTC and wanted to finish his military requirement before settling down. He had big dreams of becoming a civil engineer and seeing the world with Yancey. He was the first in his family to attend college, and his mother and big sister made sure he stayed focused. When Derrick wanted to propose to Yancey, mother and sister convinced him it was a big mistake. Yancey was devastated.

"I said he was alright, but you need to call him."

"What's the matter?"

"I'll let him explain that. You know he doesn't like me in his business. But you need to call him soon."

"I don't have his number."

"That's why I'm calling. His home phone number is 309–555–8888 and his work number is same area code, 555–9282."

"Isn't Derrick expecting my call?"

"No, but like I said, you need to call him," Mrs. Lewis said firmly.

"I will," Yancey said flatly.

"Soon."

"I will. I have to go," Yancey said. She hung up the phone without a good-bye.

1 4

I COULD TELL something was wrong when Yancey opened the door. She had tears in her eyes and even the sight of me didn't remove the mournful look on her face.

"What's the matter?" I asked as I gave her a small kiss on her forehead.

"I got a job offer. It's the lead in *Chicago*," Yancey said.

"That's great news."

"It's in Las Vegas."

"Las Vegas?"

"Yes, and it's for a month," Yancey said.

"But it sounds like a great opportunity." I tried to sound encouraging.

"Basil, I'm not talking about Philly or D.C. Las Vegas is in the middle of nowhere," she said in a heartsick voice.

"Then don't take the job. Something will come up here," I advised. It was during times like this when I didn't know what to say to my women. There were still some things I didn't understand. On the one hand I wanted to be supportive, yet I didn't want her to think I was eager to get rid of her. I gently took her hand and moved her toward the sofa.

"Do you want something to drink?" I asked as we sat down.

"No, I don't feel like anything."

"So that's the cause of the sad face. A great chance to strut your stuff in Vegas," I said and lifted Yancey's chin toward me.

"Can you come with me?" Yancey asked in a little girl–like voice.

"Baby, you know I can't do that. I mean not for the entire month. This is my busy time. I just agreed to go to Chicago in a couple of days for Brison. We're thinking about opening an office there."

"I know I'm acting like a baby, but I don't know if this is the right move," Yancey said.

"What does your agent think?"

"Who cares what she thinks?"

"You're paying her to help you make these decisions," I said.

"I know, and it is the lead."

"And you'll be wonderful."

"And you'll come and see me at least once a week, right?"

"I'll do my best," I answered. "Besides, I can always see who we have on our wish list of potential clients playing in the area. Maybe I can come once a week."

"That would be wonderful. Let me go call Lois and tell

her I'm taking the job. They needed to know right away," Yancey said with a slight edge of uncertainty in her voice.

"And I'll go pick up some California rolls and tempura. How does that sound?"

"Good," Yancey said. We both stood up holding each other's hand.

"Should I get enough for Windsor?"

"First thing, she probably doesn't know what a California roll is, and I don't think she's here."

"Oh, here is the check I promised," I said as I removed the envelope from my suit jacket and handed it to Yancey.

"You made it out to me, right?" Yancey asked, ripping open the envelope.

"No, I made it out to Hale House," I said.

Yancey looked at me and with a disgusted shake of her head said, "I've already given Windsor a check. You need to do another check and make it out to me. I'll make sure she puts the receipt in your name."

"No problem. I'll do it when I come back," I said. I gave Yancey a hug and a deep kiss and prepared to step into the chill of a New York autumn night.

I WAS A little bit uneasy when the driver pulled up in front of the Four Seasons hotel in downtown Chicago. I had met Zurich Robinson briefly after a game in New Jersey. He was an All-Pro quarterback, as well as a stunning-looking man with skin the color of a Hershey bar. We exchanged phone numbers, and though nothing ever happened between us sexually, I was convinced he swung both ways from some of the conversations we had. Today I was hoping I was wrong in thinking Zurich had enjoyed some of our late-night conversations when we talked about what we *weren't* wearing to bed. Maybe Zurich was hoping for the same thing. Maybe not.

I spotted Zurich as soon as I moved out of the revolving door and onto the marble-floored foyer. I guess he remembered me too because he gave me a huge smile and walked toward me with his hand extended. I nervously returned his smile.

"Basil Henderson. Man, long time no see. How you been?"

"Just great, dude. It's good seeing you," I said as I shook his hand and patted him on the back of his broad shoulders in a businesslike manner.

"When Brison told me I was going to be meeting with a John Basil Henderson, I was thinking, *There can't be but one John Henderson who played ball*. You were doing the commentator thing for a while, right?"

"Yeah, it was a good gig. Brought me to Chicago quite a few times for Northwestern games. You want to go up to the lobby and find the restaurant? I had my assistant make some reservations for us," I said.

"Sure, lead the way," Zurich said. He was dressed in a finely tailored dark gray suit, with a light blue shirt and maroon tie.

We located the restaurant on the main floor of the hotel, and were seated by a pretty sister who showed us to a solarium with plants, lots of light, and a view of Michigan Avenue. I was looking over the menu when Zurich asked when we planned to open our Chicago office.

"No definite date yet, but we've got to be in this city," I said.

"I know. This is a great city. When I retired from football, or shall I say when injuries forced me to call it quits, I knew this was the only place I wanted to live," Zurich said as he placed a white linen napkin in his lap.

"So how long have you been out of the league?" I asked.

"Almost three years. I spent a couple of years at Kellogg, and then went to work for World Sports Associates. It's been good, but I know I won't make partner there."

"Kellogg? That's the business school at Northwestern, right?"

"Yes, it is. I always wanted to get my MBA and it really helps when it comes to counseling players on what to do with their money—even though most of them don't want to hear about saving money until they've bought their mama and girlfriends a new car and a house." Zurich laughed. He had a nice smile, not that I was into checking out a dude's smile, which revealed perfect, sugar-white teeth.

"I heard that," I said.

"Not that I have anything against helping out your family. I built a house for my grandmother down in Mississippi, even though she spends most of her time up here with me. She fell in love with Chicago just like me."

"So how did you sign Bennie Wilson? And if we make an agreement, will he be coming with you?" Bennie Wilson was one of the top college players in the country whom we had tried desperately to sign. He liked us, I thought, but when it came time to sign on the dotted line, Bennie stopped returning my calls.

Zurich laughed. "MamaCee landed Bennie for me."

"MamaCee?"

"That's my grandmother."

"Yeah. How did she do that?"

"She met Bennie at a church convention about two summers ago. MamaCee had been assigned a roommate, and it turned out to be Bennie's grandmother, who was from Louisiana. MamaCee met Bennie and when she found out he played football, she told him he had to meet me."

"That's an amazing story," I said. "So Bennie's not one of those Jesus freaks, is he?"

"If you mean, has Bennie dedicated his life to Christ, then the answer is yes. It's one of the things we have in common besides both of us being raised by wonderful grandmothers," Zurich said confidently.

I didn't feel like getting into the church thing in the middle of the day. "So do you do a lot of traveling right now?" I asked.

"Somewhat. I've been covering Michigan, southern Illinois, and most of Wisconsin. Most of the schools I can hit by car. You guys know I want to stay in Chicago, right?"

"Yes, we know, but I think you'll need to come to New York for a while to get a feel for how we do business, and right now we all handle the West Coast. You know, places like Seattle and Los Angeles," I said. I had asked the travel question to find out what his personal situation was. Had Zurich gotten married or had he picked sides and was living with some dude? I looked at his hands and only noticed a ring like the kind players get for playing on championship teams. I guess the only way I was going to find out was to ask. I took a couple of bites of my New York strip and quizzed, "So, Zurich, are you married or something?"

Zurich finished a bite of his salmon, raised his eyebrows, and said, "I just recently ended a relationship."

I wanted to know more. "Was it a difficult separation? I know how hunnies can be when a brotha's had enough."

"I wasn't married to this person, and we're still good friends. Very good friends and let's just leave it at that," Zurich said firmly. He picked up his glass of tea, took a long sip, and glanced pensively out the large picture window.

16

YANCEY WAS brushing her hair in rhythm to "All That Jazz" from *Chicago* when the phone in her hotel suite rang. She had just finished a cool shower after eight hours of hard work, and was looking forward to a peaceful night's sleep. The dry Vegas weather and constant practicing had worn Yancey down.

"Hello."

"Darling, how is Las Vegas?" It was Ava, with whom Yancey hadn't spoken in several days. In the last couple of years, it was not unusual for Yancey and her mother to go weeks without a note or phone call. Ava was busy with her cabaret career in Europe and a new husband, a husband who had not only given her a huge diamond ring when he married her, but three stepchildren as well. *Like she knows what being a mother is about,* Yancey thought.

"Hey, Ava, where are you?"

"In Palm Springs. I got here early in the week," she said.

"How did you know what hotel I was staying at?"

"I spoke with—what's that child's name—Wendy or Wynonna? Besides, I could have just asked for the best hotel in Vegas and figured that out. Like mother, like daughter."

"Windsor. Her name is Windsor," Yancey said.

"Where did she get a name like that?"

"Something about her mother's water breaking on the bus coming back from Windsor, Canada."

"Honey, black women ain't never gonna run out of names for their children," Ava joked.

"I kinda like her name."

"Whatever, darling. What are you doing in that dreadful city, Las Vegas? Isn't it just the most gaudy city you've ever seen?"

Yancey did think certain elements of the city lacked class, like the slot machines at the airport, but she was in no mood to side with Ava. Instead she told Ava about her new starring role and how Lois had said it could lead to work on the West Coast.

"I didn't know they were doing that show in Vegas. How is the cast, and more importantly, how is your understudy?"

"The show is real popular here. You know, with all the tourists it might run forever, but I'm outta here in a couple of weeks. I've only met a few members of the cast. I might go check them out tomorrow night, but right now I'm beat. I'd forgotten how hard this show can be."

"What about your understudy?" Ava repeated.

"Oh, I did meet her, some really homely girl named Darla. The child ain't that bright. I can tell if she wasn't black, she'd be a blonde. Got a nice body and can dance, but Ava, she does that *talk singing,* so I'm not hardly worried about her. They ain't paying her twenty K a week." Yancey giggled as she gave herself a $5,000 raise.

"Watch your back. You know white folks don't mind that talk singing. Some of them don't know one note don't make a song. I can't tell you how many shows I've been in where the leading lady would talk through a song and the crowds would love it. You see it all the time when movie and TV stars decide they need to do a musical but fail to realize you have to sing!"

Yancey picked up the portable phone from the nightstand and moved over toward the large picture window facing the Las Vegas strip. The pink and orange sun was setting toward the west and the city looked like a circus midway. The producers had provided Yancey with a sprawling suite with an open dining area and a living area with a melon-color sofa and matching chair. The bedroom included a king-size maple sleigh bed, with a corn-colored velvet chaise lounge.

"When is your opening night?"

"What?" Yancey asked. She had spent a few seconds enjoying the view as Ava went on about all the parties she was going to attend while in Palm Springs.

"When is your opening? I might come out for opening night. When is it? It's been a while since I've been to Vegas," Ava said.

"They're giving me a week to get ready, even though I

know this role like the back of my hand. And my first performance isn't really like an opening night."

"I'll give you a call in a couple of days and check the
flight schedules," Ava said.

"That will be fine," Yancey said. *Like you're really going
to show up,* Yancey thought to herself. "Guess who called
me?" she asked.

"Who?"

"Charlesetta."

"Charlesetta?" Ava repeated in a quizzical tone.

"Yeah, Derrick's mother."

"What did she want?"

"Told me to call Derrick. Said it was important,"
Yancey said.

There was silence on the line for almost a minute before Ava finally said, "Don't do it. You got a nice young
man who is crazy about you. Don't go looking for trouble,
Yancey, please."

"What if he's sick or something? And besides, Basil
ain't hardly worried about Derrick. His cockiness is one
of the things I love about him."

"It ain't your problem. And if Basil *really* knew how
close you and Derrick once were, that cockiness would
be out the window."

"Yeah, I guess you're right."

"You know I'm right. Guess what?"

"What?"

"I made a date," Ava said. There was a sudden excitement in her voice.

"A date? Did you forget you're married?" Yancey asked.

"I didn't forget, and I'm just going to the gym and having coffee afterward. It's with my overnight express man. One day he showed up with a package and I told him I had just had a dream about him, but I didn't even know his name."

"What did he say?"

"He just smiled and said, 'My name is Hector.' He is so beautiful. So I told him he looked like he worked out a lot and I was looking for a new trainer. Hector then offered to work out with me until I found someone."

"What did you have on when you told him that?"

"Matching lavender panties and bra." Ava giggled.

"Do you think that had something to do with him being so helpful?"

"I hope so," Ava said.

"You better watch yourself."

"I will. Take care." Ava hung up.

Yancey went to the sitting area next to the bathroom and put on one of the fluffy white hotel robes. She picked up the phone, called room service, and ordered some tea and a house salad, without croutons, and low-fat ranch dressing on the side.

She picked up her leather bag from the desk and searched for a piece of chewing gum, when she noticed the slip of paper with Derrick's number. Yancey gazed at the number for a moment, thinking about Ava's advice. Finally, she told herself Ava didn't know shit about men. Especially the men in Yancey's life.

Yancey's hand shook as she picked up the phone and dialed the number. She felt a twinge of melancholy when she heard Derrick's voice on the answering machine, and then she felt a sharp anxiety mixed with fear. What if he were sick? What if he were married with children? When the message ended, Yancey hesitated for a moment, and when she started to leave a message, it seemed as though her voice had vanished. She couldn't speak. So she hung up. After a moment, she muttered to herself, "What am I doing?" Yancey was grateful she still had a voice.

17

STANDING IN the kitchen next to our conference room, I was stirring some cream into my second cup of coffee and thinking about Yancey. I was wondering what time she was going to be rolling out of bed before I called her. I pictured her in an oversized sweatshirt and some of the silk thong underwear we both loved. I must have been in deep thought because I didn't hear Brison walk into the small space, more like a closet than an actual kitchen. He had a smile on his face and was carrying a canned protein drink.

"Whassup, dude?" he asked.

"Cool, everything is cool," I said.

"How was Chicago?"

"It was alright. I didn't stay that long. Just met with Zurich and caught a flight back."

"No extra time to spend with the ladies?"

"You know I don't do that anymore. You got me confused with your other partner, Nico," I teased.

"I guess you're right. Sometimes I don't know how that boy ever gets any work done. Didn't you used to date some lady there?"

"Yeah, but I haven't talked to her in a while and she's probably married or some shit," I said. I opened the refrigerator and placed the cream back on the top shelf.

"Well?" Brison asked with a quizzical look on his face. He had dropped his can in the wastebasket, and his large hands were cupped and dangling by his waist. It was like he thought I could read his mind or something, knowing the answer to his unposed question. His body language looked like a question mark.

"Well what?" I asked.

"What did you think of Zurich Robinson?"

"Oh, he was cool. I actually played against him, and talked to him a couple of times after games," I said. I didn't look in Brison's eyes. Instead I looked around the counter area like I was in search of some sweetener for my coffee. I was starting to worry every time I heard his name.

"Do you think he's partner material?"

I took a deep breath. "Could be," I said, trying to sound positive.

"With all the black quarterbacks coming out of college, it sure would be nice to have a former one in our camp," Brison said.

"Yeah, I hadn't thought of that. What does Nico think?"

"He's meeting with him later this week. Then I thought we'd bring him in for some sort of final interview and make an offer or keep looking," Brison said. "All of his financial information checked out, and he's really a great guy."

"Sounds like a plan. Just let me know, but make sure it's not next Monday because it's Yancey's first show in Las Vegas. I've gotta be there front and center," I said.

"No problem. Man, do you know how your eyes just light up when you mention her name? When are you guys going to make it legal?"

"Sooner than you think, dude," I said as I winked at Brison and headed back to my office.

When I got back to my office, I asked Kendra to make plans for my trip to Las Vegas. Just before I opened the door to my office, I turned and said, "Kendra, find out who's the stage manager and producer for *Chicago* in Las Vegas. Also, call Robert, my jeweler at Tiffany's, and tell him to bring over his good stuff."

1 8

A NUMBING FEAR engulfed Yancey as she prepared to step forward and take her bow during her first night in *Chicago* as tabloid-crazed murderess Velma Kelly. After giving the chorus, principals, and her costar thunderous ovations, the audience had become eerily silent. The silence seemed as pure as a deep sleep. Yancey's eyes became as large as Christmas ornaments. Amanda, a tall, slim redhead with olive-green eyes, encouraged her to step forward. Yancey looked down toward the orchestra pit and eyed the conductor, who avoided her glance with a smirk.

Why had the audience suddenly become silent, Yancey wondered. Was she in the middle of some strange Vegas opening night tradition? Spook the star? Or had she been so awesome in her singing and dancing that she had mesmerized the audience into silent submission? Or was the mostly white audience not used to seeing a beautiful black diva play a role made famous by white actresses such as Gwen Verdon and Bebe Neuwirth? Had she missed some verses to her songs or not been as spectacular at dancing as Jasmine Guy the night before? Although Yancey had purposely avoided watching Jasmine before stepping into the role, she would put her talents as a singer and dancer on a level with anyone's.

A few seconds passed before Yancey finally stepped forward. Her whole body began to tremble as she started to eye the nearest exit. The stage manager whirled on stage and presented her with an opening night bouquet of pink roses, and a simple kiss on her cheeks, as he whispered, "You were wonderful." But still the audience was silent.

The last time Yancey had felt so unnatural after a performance was back in Memphis, Tennessee, when a high school rival had shouted out obscenities while Yancey was performing in *Dreamgirls*. A permanent restraining order had erased the fear of Nicey ever showing up in a theater where Yancey was performing.

As Yancey was forcing her best fake diva smile, she suddenly heard a male voice call out her name from the third row.

"Yancey Harrington Braxton," the voice boomed. Yancey recognized Basil's baritone voice immediately. She wanted to cry with joy when she heard him say her name. Suddenly there were houselights hovering over him, producing an almost angelic glow around his body. Dressed in a black suit, with a black shirt and silk silver tie, Basil was holding more pink roses and an aqua-blue box.

"Basil," Yancey said as she moved closer to the edge of

the stage, using her free hand to protect her eyes from the harsh stage lighting. "Is that really you?" Hours before her performance, Basil had phoned Yancey in her dressing room with bad news. He had missed his flight from New York and wouldn't reach Las Vegas until the following morning. This was going to be the first opening night he would miss since they had started dating. Yancey, though disappointed, was understanding, and told him everything would be just fine. She was relieved when Ava had also called to cancel because her husband, sick with flu symptoms, wanted Ava by his side. Yancey was so accustomed to Ava's last-minute cancellations that the only thing that caused her anxiety was when Ava didn't call and actually showed up. On those rare occasions, Ava would then spend the evening recalling her own opening nights in Europe and Japan, eclipsing Yancey's moment.

"Yes, baby, it's me. I have something I need to ask you," Basil said. He moved from his seat and walked down the aisle with a spotlight trailing him until he was a few steps behind the orchestra pit and the now smiling conductor. His face beamed brighter than the houselights, and from the way his voice was projecting, Yancey assumed he was miked.

"Will you do me the honor of spending the rest of your life with me? Will you marry me?" he asked. The question came easily, tumbling softly from his lips. Basil's handsome face looked gallant and peaceful.

Tears began to brim from Yancey's eyes as she covered her mouth in shock and slight amusement. As the tears continued to flow, Yancey began shaking her head back and forth as she shouted in her best high drama voice,

"Yes, I'll marry you!" As Basil blew her a kiss and started toward the stage, the audience and Yancey's new cast-mates broke out in cheers of "brava diva" and gave her a thunderous standing ovation. It was the loudest and sweetest applause Yancey had ever heard, for a role she longed to play: Mrs. John Basil Henderson.

1 9

YANCEY WAS standing naked as the day she was born, with the exception of the three-carat platinum diamond ring I had given her the night before. As I gazed at her beautiful body, with her breasts like ripe summer peaches, small waist, and upside-down-heart-shaped ass, I knew I had made the right move in asking her to be my wife. She was standing by the desk, with the phone in her right hand, just after we had finished making love for the third time. We had spent the first part of the evening drinking champagne, and I was smoking cigars, with several of her castmates in a private room at the casino. Then we returned to her hotel suite and made love. First in the foyer, then the living room, and finally, we reached the bedroom right before sunrise.

"Do you want some fruit on top of your waffle, baby?" she asked, looking at me with a huge smile while twirling her ring finger in the air as if it were a magical baton.

"Sure, tell them to put on some strawberries, with a little whipped cream on the side," I said.

When she finished ordering breakfast, Yancey looked at me with a sexy smile and asked, "Do you think we got time for another ride before they deliver breakfast?" I loved being with a woman who enjoyed sex as much as I did, and hoped her sexual appetite didn't change once we were married.

"I thought you wanted bacon," I teased.

"I can get bacon anytime," she smiled.

"You can get me anytime, but I think I'm out of raincoats. But we can do some other things," I said as I moved my tongue slowly from side to side on my bottom lip, letting my bride-to-be know the tongue was ready for work.

"I love it when you talk nasty, big daddy," Yancey said. She bounced on the king-size bed as if she were at a teenage slumber party. "So, when are we going to do it?" Yancey asked and laid her head on my chest.

"Right now," I said.

She lifted her head and looked at me and said, "Not that, silly. When are we going to get married?"

"When do you want to? I mean, we can do it today. We are in Sin City and I'm certain we can find one of those wedding chapels people like Dennis Rodman always seem to find," I teased.

"No, I want to get married in New York, and I want to do it before the new millennium," Yancey said firmly. "I've always dreamed of a winter wedding. And if we get married before the end of the year, it will mean I'll be married to you for two centuries."

"But that's only about a month and a half away. You think you can pull together a wedding by then?" I asked. I had always assumed Yancey would want a big Broadway production–type of wedding, complete with a big opening dance number.

"I want a small, intimate wedding, and I can always hire someone to pull it together. Windsor will help and Ava also. I just have to make sure Ava realizes it's my day and keep her from turning it into some big production. Maybe we should get married at a nice hotel in midtown or a fancy restaurant like Tavern on the Green or that place where Puffy Combs had his birthday party. I can't remember the name of it, but I tore the page out of *Vanity Fair*. I'll make sure all we have to do is show up on time," Yancey said as she pulled the sheet up around her shoulders.

"Cool by me. It's going to be your day and I want you to be happy," I said. I pushed her hair back over her shoulders and kissed her lips.

"Are you sure? Because it's your day also. I just want to enter the new century as Mrs. John Basil Henderson," she said. She gave me a small peck on the cheeks and then my lips. Yancey began to kiss my neck and my chest and was heading for my growing manhood when the doorbell rang.

"Damn, baby," I murmured. "Do you have to get that?"

"You don't want cold food, now, do ya?" Yancey asked with a sensuous smile.

Before jumping from the bed and picking up the robe from the floor, she leaned over me and whispered, "Don't worry, I'll still be hungry after we finish breakfast."

20

WHEN YANCEY called Ava to announce her pending nuptials, she didn't expect her mother to be jumping for joy. Ava didn't disappoint.

"Are you sure you want to do this?" Ava asked before Yancey could even say how happy she was.

"Yes, and we're going to do it before the end of the year," Yancey said.

"Why so soon?"

"I'm ready."

"What about your career? Just because you've done a few Broadway shows and a commercial or two doesn't make you a star, and while you're off playing house there will be plenty of divas-in-training ready to take your place," Ava advised sharply. "And you won't be young and beautiful forever."

"I know that, but I don't plan to miss a beat. Basil supports my career two hundred percent." Yancey walked over to the window. Her hotel was next to the Las Vegas Airport and as she watched the planes take off and land she felt lonely, especially talking to her mother.

"That's now. What are you going to do if he changes? Are you sure he has the means to support you?"

"What do you mean?"

"Yancey, now, honey, I know I've taught you better than that. You haven't seen his financial statements?"

"No," Yancey said as she walked over to the dining table and picked a strawberry from her leftover breakfast plate.

"Then you better—and real soon."

"How can I do that?"

"Don't worry. I know a great private investigator in New York. All you need to do is get his Social Security number and date of birth, and we can find out where all the gold is hidden. If there is any gold to be found," Ava said smugly. Yancey knew her mother was a pro when it came to finding gold. Her current husband, Stanley D. Middlebrooks, didn't look or carry himself like a multimillionaire. The former computer programmer had sold a software program he had written to Microsoft and become independently wealthy almost overnight. The first person he met on his celebratory vacation was Ava, when the two sat next to each other in the first-class section on a flight to Hawaii. When he told Ava of his recent good fortune, she made sure he didn't have to dine alone once they reached the island. And even though the fifty-something, thin, bespectacled man from Battle Creek, Michigan, wasn't Ava's type, it didn't stop her from accepting his proposal and the seven-carat diamond, which Ava picked out herself—seven days later.

"What am I supposed to do? Just ask him for the number?" Yancey asked.

"No. The number is probably on his driver's license. Just check his wallet when he spends the night and is in the shower. Or just wait until he falls asleep. Fix him a couple of drinks and fuck him real good and he'll be out for the count."

"You think that will work?"

"It should, but if that doesn't, tell him since you guys are getting married, you want to make him the benefactor on your life insurance, and you need his Social," Ava instructed. "I think I'll have my guy check medical information as well."

"Why do we need medical information?"

"Hello! You have heard of AIDS, haven't you, darling? The gay kids aren't the only ones getting it, and you can never be too safe when it comes to your health," Ava said.

"Basil is as healthy as a horse. Besides, he's not in any of the high-risk groups," Yancey said confidently.

"I'm going to say this for the last time: You need to be safe, not sorry."

"Ava, you are too much," Yancey said.

"And you'll thank me for it when I'm dead and gone. The money I plan to make off this husband will take care of me in my old age. Even though that's a couple of decades away." Ava laughed.

"Then I'll try and get the information before he leaves," Yancey said.

"Is he there now?"

"Yeah, he's here, but he's in the health club right . . ."

Before Yancey finished her sentence she recalled Basil leaving wearing a tank top and some black spandex running pants. There was nowhere to hide a wallet in the tight-fitting garment.

"Hold on just a second, Ava. I might be able to get the information right now."

Yancey placed the portable phone on mute, raced into her dressing area, and opened the closet door. There was the suit coat, a blue shirt, and some brown jeanlike pants. Yancey felt the back pockets of the pants and checked the inside of the jacket. No wallet. She turned and was facing the bathroom and spotted Basil's tan leather duffel bag where he keep all his toiletries. Yancey went into the mirrored room and there, lying right on top, was a well-worn black leather wallet. She opened it and saw about five credit cards of various colors, a health club membership, and a Florida driver's license right behind the red and white card. *What was he still carrying a Florida driver's license for?* Yancey wondered as she looked over the information. Full name, date of birth, and Social Security number.

Instead of going back into the living room, she picked up the wall phone in the bathroom.

"Ava, I got the information."

"Give it to me."

Yancey had just finished reading the nine numbers slowly and clearly when she heard the front door open.

"I've got to go," Yancey said. She hurriedly placed the license behind the health club membership card.

"I'll get on this right away," Ava said before Yancey hung up.

21

WHEN I got back from Las Vegas, the first person I called was my beautiful sister, Campbell, and told her about my new plans. She insisted on taking me to lunch at the newly refurbished Russian Tea Room on Fifty-seventh Street to celebrate.

"I have something for you from your nephew," Campbell said.

"What?"

Campbell opened her bag and pulled out a stack of photos and passed them to me. The pictures were of Cade in his Halloween outfit, dressed in a pint-size replica of my New Jersey Warriors uniform.

"Oh, man, these are great! Look at him," I said as I looked at the six photos with Cade's smile getting bigger with each photo.

"It's still so amazing to me how much he looks like you," Campbell said. I took a second look at the photos.

The waiter placed a bottle of sparkling water on the table and asked if we were ready to order. Without making eye contact I said, "Give us a little time. The boy comes from some pretty good genes," I said.

"Sure does," Campbell agreed.

"So, I can keep all of these?" I asked as I offered the photos back to Campbell.

"They are all yours. Cade insisted."

The waiter returned and we started with a midday martini. After we finished our drink and a salad, Campbell ordered a bottle of champagne, which we drank with our chicken Kiev. It was during our lemon sorbet dessert that Campbell did something that touched me deeply. It made me sad for a moment that she hadn't been in my life since day one. Campbell gave me a box beautifully wrapped in silver with black ribbon. She told me it was from her and Cade.

I opened up the box and saw a burgundy leather journal with a gold plate that had *BASIL AND YANCEY* inscribed on it. "This is nice," I said, having no idea what I was supposed to do with a book of empty pages. I'm not a diary kinda guy. I guess Campbell figured out I was clueless, so she moved close to me and whispered, "You should make the first entry before your wedding. It should be a letter to your firstborn telling him or her why and how much you love Yancey. It's a wonderful way for children to know they were loved even before they were born."

22

WHEN YANCEY was deciding who would be in her wedding party, she suddenly felt sad at the lack of women friends she had in her life. She had never really had real girlfriends and never felt safe in the company of women. She felt most women wouldn't understand some of the choices she had made and would eventually betray her trust. Being on stage, out front, was the only place she felt safe and in control.

She didn't have to worry about a matron of honor, since Ava had already placed herself in the role. But Ava felt she needed backup, so Yancey needed to think of three ladies she could stomach for a couple of days. She decided on Judith Moore, a leggy brunette she had become friendly with during her run in *Fosse*.

Judith and Yancey had shared several long lunches on matinee days and shared the same views on having too many competitive females in your life. She would ask

Basil's sister, Campbell, for the second spot. It wasn't as if they were close friends or were particularly fond of each other, but she thought it would make Basil happy. The final choice was the hard one, especially since the only other person who came to mind was Windsor. Yancey assumed Windsor would be thrilled to be a part of her special day—and she would, if she could meet some of Yancey's requirements.

Yancey called Windsor to tell her the big news. After a couple of rings, Windsor picked up the phone. She was happy to hear from Yancey and told her everything was going great at home.

"How is Las Vegas?" Windsor asked.

"Very hot and very . . . very gaudy," Yancey said.

"I know you're a big hit with the show."

"Yeah, I am," Yancey said with an air of confidence Windsor had become familiar with.

"Has Basil been there yet?"

"Yes, he surprised me with an engagement ring on my first night."

"That's wonderful. When's the big day?"

"Before the new year. That's one of the reasons I'm calling," Yancey said.

"Do you want me to help with the preparations? I'm real good with stuff like that."

"My mother is handling most of the plans, but I'm sure she would welcome the help. I really wanted to know if you'd be in the wedding party. I want you to be a bridesmaid."

"You're kidding . . . right? I'd be honored to be in your wedding. I can't believe . . ."

But before Windsor could finish her sentence, Yancey interrupted. "Of course, you'll have to lose some weight. I want my bridesmaids to be looking fierce!"

There was silence on the other end of the line for a couple of moments and then Windsor said, "Thank you, Yancey, but I can't be in your wedding if you want me to lose weight. I'm very happy with my body, and if changing myself is required . . . well, I won't do it."

Yancey was stunned, and now the silence was on her end of the line.

"Yancey, are you still there? Did you hear what I said?"

"I heard you. Maybe you can still be in my wedding. You don't have to lose weight."

"Let me get back to you," Windsor said. "I might be better in the background."

"Whatever," Yancey said, as she hung up the phone.

2 3

I HAVE NEVER understood why mofos feel the need to tell the world their business. We'd flown Zurich into New York for a formal interview. We were getting ready to offer ole boy a chance to become a partner when he said there was something he thought we should know. I thought he was going to tell us about his strong ties to the church thang, which was pretty obvious the way he peppered his conversation with "Praise God" and "The Lord did this for my life."

Brison smiled and leaned forward and said, "What do we need to know? You haven't killed your ex-wife, have you?" I figured he was trying to lighten up a conference room that had suddenly become covered with tension.

"No, I haven't killed anyone." Zurich smiled.

"Then what do we need to know?" I asked.

His voice cracked slightly as he began to speak. "About two months ago I agreed to talk to a reporter for a cover story in *Sports Today*. I think the story is going to be on the stands in a couple of weeks."

"That's great. You think you can get in touch with the reporter and tell him you're coming to work for the fastest-growing sports agency in the country?" Nico asked.

Zurich turned toward Nico and gave him a polite smile and then said, "You might not want the agency's name in this article."

"Why not?" I asked, without realizing I was getting ready to walk right into a sexual land mine.

"The story is going to be about professional athletes who are gay or bisexual," Zurich said. There was something raw in his voice. Brison, Nico, and I were completely silent, as if we hadn't heard what Zurich said, but I heard him loud and clear.

"An article on gay athletes. Why would they want to do some shit like that, and why are you in the story? Are some of the clients you're bringing with you gay? Because if that's the case, then we need to talk about this," Nico said.

"The reason I'm in the story is because *I'm* gay," Zurich said firmly. I noticed Brison glance at Zurich, looking sympathetic and nodding his head. Nico's face had a complete look of disgust, while I was feeling as if I wanted to bolt out of the conference room.

Nico stood up and said, "We need to discuss this among ourselves." He looked at me and then Brison, completely ignoring Zurich, who was seated at the end of the conference table.

"I can understand that. If you think my coming out is

going to cause the agency some problem, then I won't pursue this opportunity any further," Zurich said calmly.

"Wait a minute," Brison said to Zurich. "Let's not make any rash decisions, but we do need to talk this over." Still I remained silent. I was just looking at the artwork on the wall and wondering what I could say that wouldn't sound sympathetic or overly harsh. After a few seconds I looked at Zurich and said, "I agree with Brison. Can we get back to you?"

"Sure, no problem. Trust me when I say I understand. Doing the article was something I feel very strongly about, but I don't expect everyone to understand why I did it." Zurich stood up and grabbed his leather portfolio. "Why don't I get a hotel room and hang around a couple of days in case you fellas want to bring me back to address your concerns."

I nodded as he walked toward me and shook my hand firmly and gave me a look like we shared a secret. I didn't look at him while he shook hands with Brison and Nico. I heard Brison thank him for coming, but nothing from Nico. When the door closed, I heard Nico's voice. It was booming.

"Can you believe that shit? Man, we came this close to bringing a fag into the firm." Nico held his fingers in a gesture that looked like he was measuring some type of condiment, like sugar or salt.

"I still think he's a great candidate," Brison said.

"Are you crazy? What kind of players you think we gonna sign with a fag as a partner? Maybe he won't take a commission. Maybe all we have to do is to promise him an unlimited supply of dick, 'cause that's gotta be what he wants. Is that the kind of reputation we want for our firm? I've worked too hard to let some dick-sucking fag come in here and ruin everything."

For the next thirty minutes Nico and Brison went back and forth over the pros and cons of having Zurich as a partner. Brison pointed out his connections and the clients he would bring. Nico said he wouldn't feel comfortable with somebody who might be checking him out every time he went to take a piss or bent over to get some water from the fountain.

Nico turned to me and said, "What do you think we should do, Basil? It's obvious Brison is still in favor of bringing the fag in, and you know I want no part of this. Looks like you're the deciding vote. What's it gonna be?"

I slammed my hand down on the table and stood up and said, "I feel you, Nico, on some of the points you bring up, man. And I agree with Brison that the clients Zurich would bring with him would be great for the firm."

"What if some of them players are sissy too? Do we want to be known as a firm that caters to fags? If that's the case, we're in the wrong business. We need to start representing models and dancers," Nico said sarcastically.

"I need to sleep on this," I said. "Why don't we take twenty-four hours and then reconvene? This is very important."

"Sounds like a plan to me," Brison said as he picked up his yellow legal pad and pen. Nico just looked at Brison and me, shook his head in disgust, and said, "I ain't believing this shit."

I was feeling the same way.

2 4

AVA CALLED for the third time in one day. Since Yancey had agreed to let her mother plan the wedding, she had talked to her more often than Yancey could ever remember.

"I've found a great place for the rehearsal dinner," she said.

"Where?"

"It's a wonderful place called Laura Belle's. It's on West Forty-third between Sixth and Seventh. It will be just perfect. Then for the wedding I found a European-style hotel with a wonderful ballroom that they can arrange to look like a chapel," Ava said. "I've already reserved the honeymoon suite for the night. You kids can leave for your honeymoon the next morning."

"I know Laura Belle's. That place is large. I've been to a couple of cast parties there," Yancey said. "Don't you think it's too big?"

"I figure we should invite about two hundred people to the rehearsal-slash-engagement party and then only about one hundred to the wedding. I had to pay triple the normal asking cost because they had some other event planned. Some child's bar mitzvah. But I laid on the Southern charm and then promised to grease the reservation manager's palm and the previously scheduled event was suddenly gone." Ava laughed.

"I don't think I know two hundred people in New York," Yancey said.

"You will when I'm finished. I hired this young lady to do publicity. She assures me she will make sure you have a who's-who guest list. People like Star Jones, Juanita Jordan, Linda Johnson Rice, Russell Simmons and his wife—you know, A-list people. And then I want to invite some of the people I know in Beverly Hills and Palm Springs. Plus, you know we will invite a few people from Jackson, like the society editor of that dreadful newspaper," Ava said.

"I don't know if I want a big wedding," Yancey said, then wondered, *Where was Ava when I wanted to have a sweet sixteen party?*

"It's not really that big. Besides, you need the publicity. Just leave it all to me. Brandi, the publicist, has already talked to Jamie Brown of *Sister 2 Sister* and George Wayne from *Vanity Fair*. She also mentioned talking to someone from *Ebony* and *Essence*."

"I have always wanted my picture in *Ebony* and *Jet*." Yancey sighed.

"And your mother is going to make it happen. I won't settle for one of those little fourth-of-a-page pictures either. I'm going to get them to do a full feature like they would if it was Oprah Winfrey's wedding."

"You're having fun, aren't you?"

"The most fun I've had in a long time."

"Thanks, Ava."

"Don't thank me yet, darling. I still got a lot of work to do," Ava said and then hung up.

2 5

WHEN I got back home from the gym, I realized I wasn't going to get any sleep until I talked with Zurich. So after I showered and drank a beer, I located his cell phone number and hoped he had his phone with him. Before I could stop to think about what I was getting myself into, I was standing at a light on Fifty-sixth Street and Seventh Avenue, two blocks away from Zurich's hotel. I was more than a little nervous, so I allowed myself to be comforted by the coolness of the evening air. What was I going to say to this man I once pursued? Would he understand why I couldn't vote to make him a partner in XJI?

Zurich had answered his cell phone like he was waiting on my call. I told him I needed to speak with him about our afternoon meeting and suggested he come by my place. Zurich said he wanted to talk with me as well, but wasn't that familiar with New York. He thought it would be better if I came to him.

When I walked into his hotel, the lobby was busy with
white businessmen and young black men who looked like
rappers or professional B-boys. It was quite a contrast,
like *Wall Street* meeting *Beat Street*. I picked up the hotel
courtesy phone and asked to be connected to Zurich
Robinson's room. Again he picked up the phone quickly.

"Hello."

"Zurich, I'm downstairs. Do you want to meet me in
the bar for a drink?"

"Man, that was quick. I don't drink, and I just got out
of the shower. Why don't you come up to my room and
then we can decide."

"What's your room number?"

"I'm in 3219."

"Cool," I said.

When I reached Zurich's room I could feel tiny beads
of sweat collecting on the back of my neck. I rang the
doorbell. Zurich greeted me wearing a white hotel robe
with a mile-wide smile.

I walked into his room, which seemed crowded with
its king-size bed, desk, and small love seat.

"Have a seat," Zurich said, pointing toward the love
seat. I was wondering why he was still wearing his robe.

"Let me get dressed," Zurich said. I thought he was going to retreat to the bathroom, but ole boy just dropped
his robe on the side of the bed. He did it so quickly that I
couldn't help but stare at him. He was wearing some
white nylon underwear that revealed everything it was
probably meant to cover. He pulled a burgundy pullover
sweater over his head and then put on a pair of black
jeans. I was trying to be cool, but the sweat was now

spreading down the small of my back. Was dude trying to get me back on his team? I hoped not. But from my glance I could tell that dude was in shape, still ready for the NFL.

After a few uncomfortable seconds, Zurich sat on the edge of the bed, slapped his palms down on his jeans, then quizzed, "So what do you want to talk about?"

"Why are you doing this?" I asked.

"Doing what?" Zurich asked.

"The article. Why are you telling the world shit they don't need to know?" I asked.

"You mean, why now?"

"Yeah, I mean, man, we were ready to sign you up. You'd be so amazing for our firm, but I think this is going to be a showstopper. Everybody's not as cool as me."

"It's sort of a long story. How much time you got?"

I looked at my watch. It was 8:47. "I got a little time. Talk."

"You ever heard of a young man named Milo Bolden?"

"Milo Bolden," I said as I rubbed my chin, thinking the name sounded familiar. "Where have I heard of him?"

"He was a ballplayer. A great player out of Chicago State."

"Was?" I asked.

"Yeah, let me tell you the whole story. I met Milo at a football camp and then again later at church. We started a friendship because he was playing QB and was saved like myself. Milo was also a top student and was certain to be a top draft pick. We had talked about me representing him."

For the next hour Zurich told me the painful story of a

young man destined for success who couldn't deal with his sexuality. When Milo shared his feelings with Zurich, he had urged Milo to talk with his minister instead of telling Zurich he was gay. Milo turned to his minister, who told him to pray without ceasing and then get married immediately. Milo, a good, churchgoing young man, proposed to a young lady the minister suggested and things seemed to be back on track. The day of the wedding, with a churchful of guests, Milo put a gun to his mouth in the bathroom a few moments before he was expected to marry his bride. As Zurich told the story, I could picture the young man and for a brief moment felt the pain he was struggling with. I had been there. But it had never gotten to the point where I wanted to kill myself. If I could have talked to Milo I would have told him, "Roll with it, young brother . . . There is a way to have your cake *and* ice cream too."

"I let him down. I could have saved him," Zurich said slowly. Each of his words was packed with emotion.

I started to open my mouth to say what I was thinking but changed my mind because I didn't have a clue as to what to say. I didn't know how to comfort a man in distress. There was silence in the room and I could see tears pooling in Zurich's eyes. Finally, I spoke. "Man, you didn't put the gun in his mouth. You're not to blame."

Zurich blinked back his tears, looked at me, then asked, "If I'm not, then who is? They did the same thing to me and I should have told Milo."

"Who did what to you?"

"The church I attended for a little while. When I met you, when we were playing ball, I was dealing with questions about my sexuality. I met this guy who I cared a great deal about, but when we hooked up, it didn't feel right to me. So I turned to the Lord, who I felt directed me to this ministry in West Chicago called Change the World. At first it was wonderful. I was spending so much time in church and playing ball that I didn't have time to deal with my issues. When Minister Donald came up to me one day and told me the Lord had revealed to him the woman he wanted me to marry, I followed. It didn't seem to matter to me that Rachel was the minister's niece. I got married, and for a few months I was happy. But after a couple of more months, those feelings returned and I was miserable," Zurich said sadly.

I heaved a sigh of frustration over not knowing what to say. Zurich noticed this, so he began speaking again. "So, you see why I had to do the article? If there is another Milo out there, then hopefully he can see somebody like me and won't feel hopeless and alone."

"But this could ruin your career." Maybe he would listen to some reality.

"It might, but I've had a wonderful career. My ballplaying days are over. I got my education and my integrity, and nobody can take that away."

"How did they find you?"

"Who?"

"The magazine. I mean, how did they know you were down on the gay tip?"

"You remember the guy I mentioned who I sorta fell for?"

"Yeah."

"He's a sportswriter. He was there for me when my

marriage ended and he was there when I was dealing with my guilt over Milo. One evening we were just sitting around and he told me he had a plan as to how we could help the other Milos out there. I agreed to do it only if I wasn't the only one. He got a player from the NBA, a baseball player, a world-class Olympic track guy, and me."

"Who from the NBA?" I asked. I knew of dudes from several teams and was wondering if I was going to have to run for cover because of my own past.

"You'll have to wait for the article. I've read it and Sean did a wonderful job. His editors are talking about nominating it for a Pulitzer."

"Man, this sounds like it's going to rock the sports world," I said, shaking my head.

"So what's going on with you?" Zurich looked at me with his handsome, round face and well-shaped lips.

"What do you mean?" I asked, trying to act dumb. I knew from his tone, and the way he was looking at me, exactly what he meant.

"Are you seeing a man or a woman?" he asked firmly.

I leapt up from my seat and said, "Dude, I'm a one-woman man. Matter of fact, I'm getting married at the end of the year to a wonderful lady. I ain't got no time for hardheads," I said. I walked over to the window and pulled back the curtain. I suddenly wondered if Zurich might be checking out my ass, so I released the thin curtain and turned around to face him.

"Are you happy?"

"I'm real happy, my brother. I finally met the right lady," I said proudly.

"You know marrying won't change things."

"Zurich, look, dude, I'm marrying Yancey because I'm in love . . . mad, crazy love. I ain't running from nothing. Now, if you feel this is what you need to do to make yourself feel better, then my jock is off to you. But you might go running back to that church like a sprinter when you meet some of these—pardon my being real—fucked-up gay dudes," I said.

"Then why do I make you so nervous?"

I walked closer to Zurich, slapped him playfully on the shoulder, and said, "Dude, you don't make me nervous. You know I ain't got nothing against whatever moves you, and I think you're cool. I just don't think you'll fit in with our firm if you're going to be in parade mode with this gay stuff. I know Nico will vote against you. Brison, I don't know."

"And what about you? I was hoping once you understood why I was doing this you'd support me."

"Why would you want to be a part of a firm where some people don't want you?"

"I'm a black man. There will always be places where people don't want me," Zurich said.

"I feel ya, but I haven't decided how I'll vote," I replied.

"I think you guys got a good thing going and I'd like to be a part of it. But if you guys say no, I'll look elsewhere, or maybe even start my own firm. You guys don't want *me* as competition," Zurich said in a cocky tone.

"Do your clients know about the article?"

"Yeah."

"And how do they feel?"

"Not a one has said he's leaving. But I guess I'll have to wait until the article comes out."

"Zurich, I feel what you're feelin' and I'm going to think long and hard. But I know how athletes can be and all of them aren't as open-minded as your clients. In the end I'll have to do what's best for me. I mean, what's best for the firm," I stuttered.

Zurich shook his head as if he understood, then said, "I got another question for you."

"I'm listening."

"Are you going to invite me to the wedding?"

"Let me get back to you on that, dude," I said, and I headed for the door.

26

I T WAS a week after Basil's surprise visit and Yancey was removing her stage makeup after her performance. She was about to dip her hand into the blue jar of cold cream when she heard a knock on her dressing room door. Yancey assumed it was the director coming to tell her how pleased he was with her performance, so she tightened the sash around her robe, checked herself quickly in the mirror, and said, "Come in."

In walked Darla, her understudy, with a little girl dressed in her Sunday best, a pink and light-blue silk taffeta dress with tiny white bows around the collar. Darla still had on her costume, a black unitard from the show.

"Darla?" Yancey's face registered complete surprise.

"Hi, Yancey. You were great tonight. I have somebody who wants to meet you," Darla said as she pushed the little girl toward Yancey.

"And who might this be?" Yancey asked. She bent over and extended her hand toward the little girl.

"Tell her your name, sweetheart," Darla encouraged the seemingly shy little girl with bright, liquid brown eyes.

"My name is Mollie. Can I have your autograph?" she asked softly, handing Yancey a plastic yellow book.

"Sure, Mollie. I'd love to sign your book." Yancey took the book and looked on her vanity for the gold ink pen she loved to sign her name with.

"Are you looking for a pen? Mollie, didn't I tell you to make sure you had a pen?" Darla asked.

"No need to worry. I have a special pen," Yancey said, spotting it next to her sterling silver hand mirror.

With her back to both Darla and Mollie, Yancey noticed how much the two favored each other from their reflection in the mirror. Maybe Mollie was Darla's younger sister. Yancey turned back around and asked Mollie if she wanted to sit in her chair while she signed her book.

"Yes, ma'am," Mollie said softly.

"You sure you don't mind?" Darla asked.

"Of course not," Yancey said as she picked Mollie up and sat her in the chair.

"Thank you, Yancey. Mollie just loved you in the show," Darla said.

"That's so sweet. Is this your little sister?"

"Oh, no. Mollie is my daughter," Darla said proudly.

Yancey looked up from the autograph book to make sure she'd heard Darla correctly. "Your daughter?"

"Yes, this is my baby."

As Yancey scribbled her name with her standard "Love and kisses" inscription, a thousand questions raced through Yancey's head. Darla couldn't be more than in her early twenties and Mollie looked to be at least six years old. She wondered who kept Mollie when Darla was on the road, like most chorus performers. Where did she get the courage to continue her career while being saddled with a child?

Just as Yancey was getting ready to get answers to some of her questions there was another knock at the door. Surely this was the director, Yancey thought.

"Who is it?"

"A flower delivery for Ms. Braxton," a booming male voice said.

Yancey smiled to herself. This was the second floral delivery she'd received from Basil, and she was happy to be marrying a man so shamelessly romantic. When she opened the door, she was greeted by a large vase filled with calla lillies so tall they covered the face of the delivery man. When he handed her the bouquet, Yancey saw the face of a man she could never forget.

Yancey drew a deep breath and tried to relax her now tense shoulders and said, "Derrick. What are you doing here?" Darla immediately noticed the distress in her voice and face, so she quickly instructed Mollie to get her autograph book so they could leave.

"I'm sorry, I didn't mean to interrupt your party," Derrick said while the three adults and child tried to maneuver around one another in the small dressing room.

"Derrick, this is Darla Givens and her daughter, Mollie," Yancey said.

"Nice meeting you ladies," Derrick said, extending his hand toward Mollie. She very sweetly placed her small hand in his.

"Thanks, Yancey. I'll see you later," Darla said as she placed her hands on Mollie's shoulders and slowly pushed her toward the door. "Say 'Thank you' to Miss Yancey, Mollie," she said.

"Thank you," she said softly.

"You're welcome. I hope I'll see you again," Yancey said.

"Me too," Mollie responded with wide eyes and a gentle smile.

After Darla and Mollie left, Yancey clicked the lock on the door and turned to face Derrick. Her emotions were like a broken strand of pearls, suddenly unleashed and scattering across the hardwood floor. She was excited to see Derrick but angry as well. How dare he show up unannounced? She was wondering why after all the years of separation, Derrick was now standing only a few inches from her. Yancey's eyes filled with both curiosity and concern, while Derrick's eyes had the look of glazed excitement. She looked in heavy silence at his cinnamon-brown, clean-shaven face. After a few moments, she tried to speak, but her voice cracked when she mumbled, "I can't be—"

"Believe I'm here," Derrick finished. "I bet I'm the last person in the world you expected to see tonight. I'm in town for a conference and I saw your name on the marquee. Can't be but one Yancey Braxton." Derrick then moved so close to Yancey that his breath felt like a gust of wind. And then Yancey fainted.

PART TWO

2 7

YANCEY'S EYES jerked open in a panic. At first she didn't realize where she was and then she recognized Derrick sitting on the edge of the bed with a paper cup in his hand. He was reading a newspaper that lay open on the bed.

The night before, after Yancey had fainted, Derrick suggested she see a doctor immediately. Derrick even asked the stage manager, Talbert, if he could help locate a doctor. Yancey drank a couple of glasses of water and rested with a cold towel on her forehead for about an hour. She told Derrick and Talbert she would be fine with a good night's rest. After Talbert left, Derrick insisted that he should spend the night in Yancey's suite to make sure she was alright. Yancey was exhausted and still in shock, so she agreed to let him stay, but made it clear to Derrick that he would sleep on the sofa.

"How are you feeling?" he asked as he stood up.

"I bet I look terrible," Yancey said. She patted her hair with her hands and looked around the room for a mirror. Then she looked closely at Derrick. He looked the same as he had when he had helped her move her boxes in a rented U-Haul from the dorm when they moved into their first apartment about a mile from Howard's campus. Derrick was tall, with a solid-looking body, like a sprinter. His coarse brown hair was trimmed to military shortness and his skin was an oatmeal brown. His features were too plain for him to be considered handsome like Basil, but he had beautiful hazel-brown eyes and a boyish vulnerability that Yancey found hard to resist.

"Do you ever think about Madison?" Derrick asked.

"Madison? Who's Madison?" Yancey asked. *What is he talking about,* Yancey wondered as she pulled the sheets and comforter up close to her neck as if she were covering some horrible skin problem. She sank back to enjoy the comfort of the down pillows.

"Aw, I forgot. You didn't name her," Derrick said.

"Derrick, you're tripping. Didn't name who? Who is Madison?"

There was a heavy silence in the room as Derrick reached for Yancey's hand and rubbed it gently, then said, "Madison is our daughter."

"Our daughter?" Yancey screamed. "What are you talking about? We gave our baby up for adoption!" Suddenly Yancey was thinking back to the day when she told Derrick she was pregnant and he had firmly said, "I'm not ready for a child. I'm not ready to get married. I want to be on my feet financially before I start a family."

"*You* gave her up," Derrick corrected.

Yancey leaned toward Derrick. "*We* gave her up—where were you? But tell me what you're talking about. I don't know any Madison," Yancey said as she began shaking her head from side to side in disbelief.

Her mind wandered back to those college days in Washington, D.C. She had discovered she was pregnant a month after Derrick started to waver about their future. Yancey's first reaction was to have an abortion. If she couldn't have a life with Derrick and their child, then she'd devote herself to her career and becoming a star. When Derrick overheard Yancey talking to Ava about scheduling an abortion, he pleaded with Yancey to let him do the right thing despite his own family's objections. Several months after accepting Derrick's proposal, Yancey decided Derrick's offer had more to do with his guilt than true love. When she confronted him, Derrick confirmed her suspicions. She couldn't start off their life like that. But it was too late for an abortion, so Yancey decided the best thing for their unborn child was adoption, and broke off the engagement just weeks before she delivered the baby.

"I couldn't give her up. She was my blood. When I went to the lawyer's office to sign the papers, something just came over me. I don't know if it was guilt, and even though I know I wasn't ready to be a parent, I also knew I couldn't just let her go out in the world without knowing who her father was. So I arranged for my sister, Jennifer, to adopt her. Jen wanted children really bad and when she approached me with the idea . . . well, it just seemed like the right thing to do. She has been a great mother."

"Then what's the problem? Why are you here? And why are you telling me this?"

Derrick's eyes suddenly filled with tears and he began to cry uncontrollably for about five minutes. As he slowed his crying and rubbed his eyes with his large hands, he said, "Jennifer is dying. She can't be Madison's mom anymore, and Jen said Maddie needs a mom after she's gone."

The room fell silent again. For Yancey the silence felt suffocating, as though someone had taken a pillow and was trying to smother her. Yancey walked over to the window, opened the curtains, and looked at the hazy morning sky, the clouds struggling to cover the sun. She then closed her eyes, commanding herself to breathe deeply so that she could wake up from this living nightmare, but she could still hear Derrick's voice.

"My sister has cancer. Breast cancer, and this is her second bout. The doctor said she probably has about three months to live. It was Jennifer's suggestion that I contact you. At first I didn't think it was such a good plan. But I thought, what if you want to see your daughter one day? Maybe one day when it is too late. Jennifer never married, but she is seeing a guy who loves her crazy. But he hasn't been a father to Madison. That's been my job. Even though I never considered it a job. She's a joy."

Yancey remained silent.

Derrick finally asked, "Yancey, are you alright? Do you understand what I said?" He spoke in a low, soothing voice. He walked over to the window and put his arms around Yancey's waist. His touch seemed to release the tension in her body. After a few minutes Yancey pulled herself from Derrick's embrace and turned around to face him.

"Please tell me this is some kind of sick joke. Please . . . please."

"I can't do that. Our daughter is very much a part of my life and my family. I'm here to see if you want her to be a part of yours. Are you ready to be a mother?"

"Are you out of your mind? This is as close as I have ever been to happiness. I'm getting married!" Yancey yelled as she pushed her ring finger in Derrick's face. Her voice sounded erratic and uneven.

"Who is the lucky guy?"

Yancey wanted to slap Derrick silly. "Is this why your mother called me? Why didn't she tell me about the child? What did you say her name was?"

"I was upset with her for calling. It wasn't her place. And her name is Madison. Jennifer named her Madison. It fits her to a T. Would you like to see a picture of her?" Derrick asked as he reached in his back pocket and pulled out his wallet.

"No! Don't do that. I don't want to see a picture of somebody I don't know," Yancey said.

As Derrick placed his wallet back in his pocket, he noticed the haunting look of sadness in her eyes and the large, effortless tears that were now flowing down her face. He was coming to the gut-wrenching realization that very soon, his daughter would be without a mother.

2 8

I WOKE UP in the middle of the night with my body soaked with sweat and my jimmie rock hard. Both of these things disturbed me deeply. I had awakened from a dream—make that nightmare. I usually don't remember my dreams or think they mean anything, but this one was different. It was a sexual dream with Zurich and myself, doing things that required breaking the laws of gravity. The scary part of the dream was that I was really feelin' him until Yancey stepped into the room of my dream. All I remember is her screaming "Get off him, you asshole," and shaking her head from side to side as if she were possessed. It wasn't clear if she was yelling at me or Zurich. It was some strange shit. Maybe Zurich was trying to tell me what might happen if I voted against making him a partner.

I decided the only thing that could take my mind off Zurich and his cucumber-size jimmie was some phone sex with my baby. I picked up the phone and dialed her number as I felt my jimmie become as limp as wet celery. But I knew once I heard her voice it would be back standing at full attention.

After a couple of rings, I asked the hotel operator for Yancey Braxton's room as I reached over to my nightstand and pulled out my favorite lubricant. As the phone continued to ring, I put a little of the greasy substance in the palm of my hand and prepared to take my jimmie to ecstasy. All I needed was to hear the sexy, sweet voice of my angel, but instead I got a hotel recording informing me that the guest wasn't available and to leave a message. I started to hang up, but instead I whispered in my best *I want to knock some boots* voice, "Hey, sweet lady. This is your man. I was holding on to something here that misses you dearly. Now what am I gonna do? Where are you? Call me." I hung up the phone and started to take matters into my own hands, literally. I imagined Yancey lying on a bed of white rose petals with a body-clinging natural-colored nightgown. Her hair was perfect, framing her beautiful face like a silk scarf, and she had a finger in her mouth, softly sucking on it as if it were some exotic delicacy. Even with this picture in my head my jimmie remained unimpressed, and for a second I thought back to my dream with Zurich, and this made me feel even more uneasy. I was through with that kinda shit.

The next morning I jumped out of bed and was heading for the shower when I had a brilliant idea. I returned to my bedroom, picked up my phone, and called my travel agent. I told her to get me on the first flight going to Las Vegas. She asked me if I could make a flight four hours later. I told her I was there. It was obvious to me that I needed something more than phone sex before I got myself into some kind of trouble I didn't even want to think about.

I was on my way out the door, garment bag in hand, when I heard my phone ring. My first thought was that it was Yancey calling me back, but my caller ID showed a number from my office. It had to be either Nico or Brison.

"Hello."

"B, whassup?" Nico asked.

"On my way out the door, dude. Going to see my lady for a night or two."

"Didn't you just get back from Vegas?"

"Yeah."

"Now don't tell me you ain't got a little something stashed away here in the city for times like these," Nico joked.

"You know my player days are over, so I'll leave the playin' up to you. And I know you didn't call me to discuss my love life."

"Naw, dude. Man, I need you on my side. I get the impression that old goody-two-shoes Brison is going to vote to let that faggot in the firm. And B, you know that's going to hurt us. Dude, everybody in the business will be talking and laughing at us when this damn article comes out if we bring him on board. This shit has got my dander up big time," Nico said.

"I feel you, man. But what makes you so sure he's going to vote to bring him in?"

"Trust me, I know him. He's family and I love him, but I don't think he's thinking straight. I mean, he keeps talking about all the business this dude will bring with him, but I think between the three of us, we can get his clients and then some."

"How you figure?"

"B, I bet you cash money that his big-name clients don't know they're dealing with some church-goin' fag. I think he's just bluffing. I know if we talked to his clients and laid out what we could do for them . . . they would sign with us quicker than a crack whore minute."

I looked at my watch and realized I needed to head toward the airport. I started to tell Nico about my conversation with Zurich and how I didn't think he was going to come on board unless it was a unanimous vote, but then I figured I didn't want any questions on why I was talking with him one on one.

"Maybe he will ask to take his name out of consideration," I offered.

"Where else is he going to go? What you wanna bet them white boys have already showed his ass the door? Where else is he going to find fresh dick unless he's patrolling the locker rooms all over the country with cards that have our company's name on them?"

Again I started to come to Zurich's defense. I didn't know a lot about him, but I knew he wasn't the type to mix business with pleasure. That sounded more like Nico and my former self.

"Dude, like I said, I feel you, but can this wait until I get back from Vegas? Ain't nothing going to happen until we vote, and who knows, Brison might change his mind.

He might realize we don't need to take on another partner."

"I hope you're right, man. But if we got to have somebody gay in the firm, then let's get some pussy-eatin' dyke in here. At least with a bitch like that we might get a chance to watch," Nico joked. At least it sounded as if he was joking. With Nico you could never tell.

"Dude, my car is waiting downstairs. I've got to bounce," I said.

"Be safe, dude, and hit that stuff for me."

"I'll holler at you when I get back, Nico."

2 9

DERRICK TOOK Yancey's hands and said very softly, "I know this is an awful lot to drop on you. And I know we are very different people from when we were back at Howard. I regret some choices I made. It looks like you have the career you've always wanted and you tell me you're happy. But I want you to think about this very seriously. I think we can make this work. We can turn this bad situation into something positive."

It was midafternoon and the two were sitting on the sofa in the living room of Yancey's suite. They had spent the night in Yancey's bed, holding each other tightly, as they had done so many nights in their apartment near Howard, Derrick's chin resting gently on the top of Yancey's head. In those days the music of Sade and Luther Vandross would play in the background when they made love. But the previous night there was no music or lovemaking, simply two people holding each other for comfort. Yancey was thinking about how a child she didn't know would drastically change her life and future. She kept asking herself if she could ever be a good mother when she had had such a poor example in Ava. Would it be best that Madison didn't have a mother rather than someone poorly equipped to provide the love a child deserved? What would become of her relationship with Basil, and could she love Derrick so strongly again?

The morning found them sharing toasted bagels with grape jelly and black coffee. After breakfast, Yancey and Derrick went for a run in the gym, for the most part in total silence, a silence that seemed as pure as air. They didn't seem to notice the few patrons milling around the weights, even when an overweight white man got on the treadmill next to Yancey and tried to strike up a conversation. Whenever Derrick tried to bring up Madison, Yancey protested, cutting her eyes at him. Derrick nodded back at her in a solemn agreement to discuss their problem later.

When they returned to the suite, the silence continued for a few minutes until Derrick called out, "Yancey?" When she turned suddenly to face him, Derrick paused and pursed his full-lipped mouth as if to whisper. He moved from the bedroom's french doors and took a seat on the sofa. Yancey remained silent while gazing into Derrick's eyes as though she were in some type of trance. After a few minutes he began to speak again. "I guess what I want to say is . . . maybe we ought to think about getting married. What do you think?"

"What are you talking about?" Her voice was thin and

wavered a bit. "I'm already getting married. You think I'm just wearing this ring for my health?" Yancey asked as she flashed her ring finger directly in his face. A memory of Basil down on his knees in the theater flashed through her mind as she raised her voice in sadness and anger.

"Do you love him?" Derrick asked.

"Do you love me?"

Derrick was silent for a few moments and then added, "I loved you once very much. I love Madison to death. You are a part of her, and I think I could learn to love you again."

"Learn to love me again? You are really trippin' now. I think it's time for you to leave," Yancey said. "I've seen this movie and I know how it ends."

Derrick got up from the sofa and took Yancey's hands and said, "Please think about this. I'll call you before I leave tomorrow." He leaned forward and kissed her softly on her cheek. Derrick grabbed his tan leather garment bag and began to walk out of the suite when Yancey shouted, "Wait!"

Derrick turned around and asked, "Wait for what?"

Yancey moved closer to him and said, "Since you didn't see the show the other night, do you want to come tonight?" *Maybe if he sees me on stage,* Yancey thought, *he'll realize what he's asking me to give up.*

"Sure, I'd like that. I'm done with my business here."

"I'll leave you a ticket at the box office. Come to my dressing room after the show. Maybe we could talk some more."

"Cool," Derrick said as he moved closer to Yancey and

kissed her forehead. After his lips lingered a moment he opened the door and walked into the hallway.

A few minutes after Derrick left, Yancey suddenly felt cold, as if she were locked in a room even the sun could not warm.

I EXPECTED YANCEY to be surprised when I knocked on her dressing room door. But it was me who got the surprise. Right as I walked up to her door I could hear voices. It was Yancey and a male voice, and although their voices were muffled, I heard Yancey asking if there were any more surprises, and a male voice with a lot of bass replied, "No." Then there was a prolonged silence, so I knocked on the door. "Come in," Yancey said. I opened the door, which was unlocked. There she was, sitting at her dressing table in her robe with some mofo sitting nearby on the sofa with his legs crossed. When I walked in carrying a dozen pink roses, she smiled and pulled her robe together, then got up and gave me a halfhearted hug and a quick kiss.

"What are you doing here? I mean, you didn't tell me you were coming. But what a wonderful surprise," she said.

I eyed ole dude sitting on the sofa and quizzed, "Am I interrupting something?"

Yancey looked at him and then unleashed a sudden rush of words. "This is just my day for surprises. This is Derrick. Derrick Lewis. You remember me mentioning him? Derrick from D.C., who now lives in California . . . which is close to Vegas. He was just in town on business and he surprised me right before the show, a half hour before curtain, and I invited him to the show and backstage afterward."

I thought, *Shouldn't he be waiting outside the theater and not in your dressing room?*

Derrick stood up, extended his hand, and said, "Whassup, guy? Yancey has told me a lot about you."

I replied, "Same here," but I was wondering, *When did she tell him about me? During intermission, or has he been communicating with my lady before tonight?* I maintained my cool. I kept my arm around Yancey's waist tightly while eyeing ole dude. I glanced at her dressing room table and noticed she still had a picture of me, looking great with no shirt and a pair of jimmie-revealing swim trunks. But I also noticed a vase of flowers I didn't send.

"Isn't this just wonderful?" Yancey said with an uneasy quality in her voice. It sounded as though she felt ashamed of something. I knew it couldn't be. Ole boy was decent-looking, but he couldn't touch me. She removed my arm from her waist and said, "Let me take a quick shower. Derrick and I were going to get something to eat. How does that sound, baby?"

Before I could respond, Derrick spoke. "Yancey, you

can give me a rain check. I don't want to be a third wheel."

"Okay, that's fine. It was good seeing you," Yancey said as she extended her hand toward Derrick. "Tell your mother I said hello, and I'll put your sister at the top of my prayer list." She smiled. Prayer list? I didn't even know Yancey prayed. I noticed a nervousness in her smile that made it appear fake, like some beauty queen grinning at her runner-up, thinking, *Aren't you so happy for me?*

"I will," Derrick said as he gave Yancey a half-assed hug and then moved out like a wounded puppy. There was a feeling in the room that I had spoiled some big plans.

When Derrick left, Yancey gave me another hug and a deep kiss, which I wasn't exactly feelin'. She picked up on it and looked at me and asked, "Basil, are you alright?"

"I'm cool. So what was dude doing in town?"

"He was up here for a convention. He's an engineer for Hughes Aircraft right outside of L.A. He came to tell me his sister was sick with cancer. Derrick is really down about it," Yancey said.

I started to ask if that was the surprise or couldn't he have told her that on the phone, when Yancey noticed a hotel card key on the sofa and said, "Oh, Derrick left his key. I've got to catch him." I was going to offer to track him down myself, but she was suddenly out of the room, still in her robe and moving as if she were in a jailbreak. In the two years I had known her I had never seen Yancey appear so nervous or move so quickly. Something was up, and I had a feeling I wasn't going to like it.

31

AFTER DERRICK and Basil left Las Vegas, Yancey felt both alone and powerless. She was suffering from emotional exhaustion and her heart was filled with a mixture of happiness and horror. She felt joy that the man she had once dreamed of spending her life with was now suggesting she do just that. Despite her strong feelings for Basil, she couldn't keep from reliving the memories of her love for Derrick. Yancey didn't know what to do, so she called Ava.

It was a couple of hours before she had to be at the theater when she dialed her mother's home number. A maid informed Yancey that Ava was in New York and could be reached on her cellular phone. Yancey hung up and quickly dialed the second number.

"Hello," Ava said as she stepped out of her limo. At forty-five, Ava was still in her prime and could still get out of a car gracefully even while wearing a tight leather skirt and five-inch heels. She dressed and carried herself like a woman who was very comfortable being noticed. If Tina Turner could wear it, so could Ava. A striking five foot seven and about 125 pounds, Ava could go down to 115 if needed in a matter of weeks, with the help of diet pills her doctor would prescribe without question. Ava didn't like to perspire, so exercise was out of the question. She wore her hair in a very short, stylish cut made popular by Angela Bassett in the movie *Waiting to Exhale*. Ava had not bought into the distinguished look of God's frosting mixed with her natural dark-brown color, so she kept her hair jet black with weekly visits to the Elgin Charles Salon.

"Where are you?" Yancey asked.

"Walking into my hotel," Ava said. Yancey could hear static and the sounds of the city in the background, and suddenly wished she was back in New York City.

"I didn't know you were going to New York," Yancey said.

"I had to get up here to plan your wedding. I could only do so much from Cali. How are you doing?"

"Not so good," Yancey responded with sadness in her voice.

"Well, I got some news that might cheer you up. I got the information I was seeking, and Basil will do just fine for a first husband. Ole boy some assets, excellent credit, and that business of his isn't doing so bad. Plus he's got some property in Florida and some mutual funds that are doing quite well."

"That's nice," Yancey said in a far-off voice.

" 'That's nice'? Is that all you can say? What's the matter with you?"

"I wish I could tell you this in person, but I need your advice. Maybe you should call me once you get settled."

"Is it bad?"

"Could be."

"Then you need to tell me now. I'm walking into the hotel right now. I'll just find someplace in the lobby before I check in."

"I can call you back."

"No, tell me what's the matter," Ava demanded.

Yancey exhaled a long, slow breath, but nervousness stuck in her voice. "How do you feel about being a grandmother?" she quizzed.

"No! Yancey, please tell me you're not pregnant."

"I'm not pregnant."

"Then what are you talking about?"

"Remember my last year at Howard when I was pregnant?"

"Yeah, that would have been the worst mistake of your life. I'm so glad you took care of that," Ava said in a dismissive tone of voice.

After a moment of silence, Yancey said, "I didn't take care of it."

"What!" Ava yelled. "I sent you the money! You told me you had an abortion. How could you have been so stupid? How could you keep this from me? I'm your mother!" There was a bitterness in her voice. Ava located a comfortable chair off the lobby of the hotel and listened to her daughter in a dazed silence.

Yancey told her about deciding against the abortion and instead giving up the child for adoption. She then shared Derrick's recent announcement as she wept intermittently through the story. When she finished, Yancey asked in a desperate voice, "What am I going to do?"

Ava's voice was firm. "You're not going to do anything different. You're going to marry Basil. Derrick and that child can go on with their lives. It is not your problem. Derrick made a choice and you made one. Now you both have to live with it. I can't believe that boy was so stupid as to believe he could raise a child. And what in the hell are you going to do with some child who you don't know and who doesn't know you from a hole in the wall?"

"But that's my child. I'm so confused," Yancey said. She flung her free hand in the air, moved up a few steps, and then backed up and leaned against the wall.

"There is no reason for confusion. As far as you are concerned that child is dead."

"Should I tell Basil?"

"Hell no! Why do you want to do that? Didn't you just hear what I said about the child being dead?"

"But she's not dead! And what if somebody finds out about her and leaks it to the press? It could ruin my career if I turn my back on her."

"You've already turned your back on her, and nobody's told the press yet. Derrick's not threatening you, is he?" Ava removed her sunglasses as if she could make Yancey see her point more clearly as she glared into the phone.

"No."

"Then why do you want to tell anybody? Especially the man you're going to marry?"

"So he can make sure he still wants to marry me," Yancey cried.

"First thing is, you don't want to give a black man

options or multiple choice," Ava said in an emotionless voice.

"What if Derrick wants to marry me?"

"Yancey!" Ava screamed. "Listen to me. Derrick had his chance and he fucked it up. You have a wonderful life. You have to forget about that child. It's over. Let it go. Move on!"

"But I've thought about that day every day since it happened! I've tried to block it out, but I can't. Until I talked to Derrick, I didn't even know if I had given birth to a boy or a girl. Ava, I have a daughter."

"You don't have a daughter, Derrick does. Do I need to come out to Las Vegas and slap some sense into you? Forget about that child. We've got a wedding to plan. And you need to keep this shit to yourself and make sure Derrick does the same. What does he want? We can come up with some money to keep that mouth of his shut."

"Derrick doesn't want any money. He said he just wanted a mother for his daughter."

"Children grow up without mothers every day," Ava said coldly.

Her words cut through Yancey's heart, and the pain was so sharp that all Yancey could do was to hang up the phone. "Damn straight a child can get along without a mother. I did!" she said out loud as she looked at her puffy eyes in the mirror. Yancey picked a few pieces of ice out of the bucket located near the bar and placed them in a linen napkin. The cold pack would get rid of the puffiness. Yancey had to pull herself together quickly. She had a show to do.

32

LOOKS LIKE I'm off the hook for a minute. When I got back from Las Vegas I stopped by the office to review my mail. I was on my way out the door and I bumped into Nico, who was smoking a cigar and had a big smile on his face. I asked him why he was so happy and Nico told me, "The fruit decided he didn't want to mix it up with us."

"Are you talking about Zurich?" I asked.

"Yeah, who else?" Nico asked as he blew a smoke circle opposite my direction.

"When did this happen?"

"He called Brison about noon today and said he decided to strike out on his own. I wonder how that shit is going to turn out," Nico joked.

"So, I guess we'll start looking for another partner."

"I guess so. But since Brison wants to be so liberal toward fags, we should go for a dyke," Nico said. He walked toward his office still puffing his cigar.

. . .

I went to the gym to work out some of the stress I was feeling. It didn't help. While running on the treadmill my
thoughts went from Yancey to Zurich. Was she playin' me?
Did he have a pull on me? Why was I worried about my future with Yancey, or if I was going to hear from Zurich anytime soon? Yancey had tried hard to reassure me when I
asked her if she still had any feelings for Derrick. When we
got to her suite I tried to see if there were any signs that
Derrick had done more than check out Yancey's performance on stage. I counted the condoms she kept in a small
brass container. There was still one packet of three. The
toilet seat was down, and I lifted it up to make sure there
was no yellow ring of piss from someone standing up, but
that would have been hard to tell since I could tell the
maid had been there to leave fresh towels and soaps lining
the bathtub. When I asked Yancey where Derrick was staying, she very quickly replied she didn't know. Her voice
sounded shaky. Once we got in bed, Yancey's hands went
straight for the jimmie. Normally I like it when she's aggressive like that, but that night I kept thinking about the
look on her face when I walked into her dressing room.
Yancey asked me if everything was alright and I told her I
was just tired from the time change and all. The next
morning when I woke up we made love, but without my
normal passion. Yancey didn't seem to notice. It seemed as
though she had something on her mind as well.

Right before I went to bed the phone rang. It was
Zurich. After we exchanged our whassups he asked,
"Have you spoken with Brison?"

"No, I went to Vegas to check on my fiancée and when I got back to the office he was gone," I said.

"Then you haven't heard?"

I told Zurich Nico had relayed the information.

"I don't think that dude feels me," Zurich said.

"What makes you say that? Nico is cool."

"I just get that feeling. But that's not why I called."

"So you're going to give it a try on your own. Maybe I'll see you out there in the trenches."

"Yeah, maybe. I'm looking forward to being on my own, and I think there is enough business out there for everybody."

"Yeah, you're probably right."

We talked for a few more minutes and Zurich suggested we keep in contact and I told him that was cool, even though I knew we weren't going to be tight.

"So when is the big day?"

"Right now we're looking at the last Sunday in December."

"That's soon. Are you ready?"

"What do you mean? Damn skippy I'm ready." There was a brief silence and then Zurich hit me with a low blow. "You know, marrying a woman doesn't change who you are. You know that, don't you?"

What in the fuck did he mean by that? I could feel my neck starting to burn like a hot iron and I was thinking it was a good thing we weren't standing face to face 'cause I would have busted him upside his head, but instead I said, "No, marrying a woman didn't change *you*." And then I hung up without a fuckin' goodnight.

33

DARLA WAS mildly surprised when Yancey invited her for a late supper after the Thursday night performance. But she really didn't know what to think when Yancey suggested one of Las Vegas's top restaurants, Très Jazz, located in the Paris Casino Resort.

After the two of them were seated, a waiter approached them to ask if they wanted anything to drink.

"Oh yes, let me have a cosmopolitan," Darla said.

"I'll just have a chardonnay," Yancey said.

Before leaving, the waiter told them about the specials of the restaurant, which was known for its New World Caribbean cuisine and continental fare.

"Let's have an order of the jerk chicken wings for an appetizer," Darla said. She looked quickly at Yancey, then asked, "That's okay, isn't it?"

"Sure, knock yourself out."

The two ladies admired the beautifully decorated

space, with its collage of arresting colors that created a warm and inviting eatery. The overhead lighting cast a buttery glow over art deco furnishings and the oil paintings of musicians adorning the walls.

"This place is beautiful," Darla said as her eyes scanned the room. "Didn't I read somewhere the chef is a black woman?"

"I think so. I know it's black-owned, which is kind of surprising in this town. I'm so sick of seeing and hearing the sounds of slot machines. Not to mention all these fashion-challenged tourists with their wash and wear pants suits and floral shirts," Yancey said.

The waiter returned with their drinks and took their order. After Darla had taken a sip of her drink, she told Yancey how surprised she was by her dinner invitation.

"Why is that?" Yancey asked.

"Well, you know, I did a couple of shows in New York and almost every tour. And you know how the kids talk," Darla said.

Yancey raised her eyebrows and asked, "What does that have to do with two new friends having dinner?"

"I just heard you weren't that social when it came to chorus members."

"It's not that. I just think that if you associate yourself with the chorus, then that's all you'll ever be. It's not that I have any problems with individuals; it's that I'm a leading lady and so that's all I see." Yancey picked up her glass of wine and took a sip.

"Then why this dinner?" Darla asked a little impatiently before she added, "Do you think I'm a leading lady type?"

Yancey wanted to say, "Honey, are you kidding?" but she needed something from Darla, so she decided to use a little diplomacy.

"You're my understudy, which means the producers see you as a person with potential."

"You think so?"

"Of course. Why else would they choose you?" Yancey knew enough to fudge a little on what she actually thought of Darla's talent if she wanted some honest answers.

"I guess I should be thanking you."

"Thanking me for what?"

"You're a trailblazer. I mean, taking over a role most people would consider a part only for a white actress. I'm so happy when I see women like you, Vanessa L. Williams, Stephanie Pope, and Diahann Carroll doing roles created for white females," Darla said.

"I guess you're right. I've always wanted to do the great roles and to create new ones. I plan to do that with film as well. Do you like old movies?"

"Oh yes. I love *Claudine, The Wiz,* and *Lady Sings the Blues.*"

"I'm not talking about those movies. Those aren't old movies. I mean the classics like *All About Eve, Mildred Pierce,* and *The Women,*" Yancey said.

The waiter placed grilled lamb chops in front of Yancey and marinated grouper before Darla, who bowed her head and said a silent prayer. Yancey thought, *Is everybody I meet into the Jesus thing?*

Yancey took a small bite of the lamb chops and placed the fork and knife on the side of the plate. "Darla, can I ask you something?"

"Sure," Darla said as she took another bite of the grouper.

"Why did you have a child? I mean, didn't you think it would get in the way of your career?"

Darla took the fork out of her mouth as a wave of shock crept over her face.

"I had a child because I was in love, and I never thought about my career or what having a child would mean."

"You didn't? I mean, isn't it hard?"

"Yancey . . . news flash: Life is hard. You deal with it. I was very much in love with Mollie's father, and I knew it was the right thing to do. Although things didn't work out with him, I got Mollie, and it's a decision I've never re-gretted."

"But how do you manage? It looks like you do a lot of road shows, so I'm assuming you're not in one place for a long time."

"My mother helps out a lot, and Mollie spends half of the year with her father, Vincent. We decided not to get married, but we're still good friends."

"And you feel that being a mother doesn't get in the way of your career?"

Darla suppressed a smile and said, "Oh, I see what this is about. You're pregnant."

"What? I'm not pregnant!" Yancey insisted. "And lower your voice! That's how rumors get started."

"Okay. But this all makes sense. The wonderful pro-posal from your honey and now this."

"I don't know if I'll ever have children," Yancey admit-ted. "Was Mollie unplanned?"

"In a way, but I haven't regretted it one second. I considered marrying Vincent, and he wanted to, but I just didn't think I loved him as much as I should. Now since I love him dearly as a friend we've created a wonderful, loving environment for our child."

"Do you plan to try and go back to Broadway?"

"Sure. I plan to audition for whatever's available when my contract is up here. It's a little easier for me in New York because I have family in the Bronx, and I have several friends in the business who've known Mollie since she was just a thought. That child has more godparents than one child should ever have," Darla said with a smile.

The two ladies savored the rest of their meal in silence. Then suddenly Windsor's refusal to lose weight popped into Yancey's mind.

"I got something else to ask you," Yancey whispered, leaning into the table, as if they were best buddies now.

"Sure, but can I get another drink?"

"Of course."

Darla motioned the waiter and ordered another cosmopolitan. Yancey shook her head "no" at the waiter.

"Would you like to be in my wedding?"

Darla's eyes snapped wide open, as though they were going to pop out of their sockets.

"You're kidding, right?"

"No."

Darla just stared at Yancey for a few seconds, then said, "Yancey, trust me, I am really honored that you would ask me to be a part of such a special day. But we don't know each other that well. Don't you have friends in New York that would love to be in your wedding?"

"Yeah, I do. But I thought this might be a way for you to be viewed as a leading lady. I mean, Basil is a big former football star, and with me having done almost every show on Broadway, my wedding is going to be a big media event. It couldn't hurt your career."

"You might be right," Darla said, then took a sip of her drink.

"Think about it. Just let me know in a couple of days," Yancey said as she placed her credit card on the table. The waiter immediately picked it up.

"Weren't you close friends with Nicole Springer?"

Yancey was startled at the unwelcome memory of the woman she had sabotaged while serving as her understudy.

"You know Nicole?"

"Yeah, I was in the *Dottie* workshop with her. She's really beautiful, and boy, can she sing," Darla said.

"What ever happened to that workshop?"

"They ran out of money, but I heard it might be getting started again, with Nicole. You know she just had twins, don't you?"

"Twins? No, I didn't know," Yancey said as she looked around for the waiter. Darla's news on Nicole had brought back her thirst.

"Yeah, she had two little boys."

Yancey got the waiter's attention and ordered another white wine.

"Sure, I can get that, but your credit card was declined. Do you have another card you can use?" the waiter asked.

Yancey looked at the waiter with a stunned look on her

face. "No! Forget the wine. I'll just pay cash," she said. She jerked her bag open and pulled out three twenty-dollar bills and laid them on the table.

"Yancey, I can split this with you," Darla offered.

"Honey, put your money back. I guess the mail moves slow between here and New York," Yancey said, referring to the credit card payment she hadn't sent. Darla opened her purse and pulled out a tin of mints to offer Yancey one. Yancey politely refused. She was still fuming from the credit card rejection.

"You know, Yancey, this has really been a treat. You are so full of surprises."

"Honey, you have no idea."

34

YANCEY HAS decided on a wedding party of four, which means I've got to come up with a best man and three groomsmen. I've decided on my dad for best man. Even though he f'd up big time with my mother, I have no doubt that he loves me. I'm going to ask Campbell to let Cade be my pint-size groomsman. He's like me and will appreciate an opportunity to dress up and be around a bunch of pretty ladies. Brison will probably make the cut, because I just think he's not only a smart business-man, but an all-around cool dude. It's the fourth spot I'm having a problem with. It's made me realize I don't have time for knuckleheads. Gay or straight. There is an argu-ment for Nico, simply 'cause if I ask Brison I don't want Nico to feel left out. Dude is so incorrect when it comes to shit like weddings. I can see him at the bachelor party, carrying on like he doesn't have any sense and talkin' shit. Besides, I know Nico doesn't give a shit about the institution of marriage. He would be like the light-skinned dude in one of my favorite movies, *The Best Man,* talkin' loud and saying nothing.

There is one person that just keeps coming into my mind. A niggah I want close by when I pledge my love to Yancey. For some reason I want to be able to look at him out of the corner of my eye when I say "I do." My dude, Raymond Winston Tyler. There is only one problem: I'm more nervous about asking Raymond to be in my wedding than I was asking Yancey to marry me. Now, ain't that some shit?

A week had passed since Derrick's big surprise, and Yancey was doing everything in her power to block out Derrick and Madison and concentrate on finishing the Vegas run in a flourish. On stage she stood out like a burst of red in a black-and-white photo. But when the curtain dropped, Yancey would become seriously depressed and couldn't wait to close her eyes and let sleep claim her.

Yancey was on her way to the theater when her cell phone rang.

"Hello?"

"Where are you?" Ava asked.

"Waiting for the elevator."

"I'm glad I caught you. I got some great news!"

"What?"

"First, I talked to my lawyer and you don't have any responsibility when it comes to Derrick and that child. If you signed away your rights before you gave birth, then that's the—"

"Ava, is that why you're calling me? I told you I don't want to talk about this anymore until I make my decision," Yancey said as she stepped onto the elevator.

"You already made your decision when you signed those papers."

"I can't hear you. I'm losing you," Yancey said. She pushed the red "end" button on her phone and dropped it into her leather bag.

35

HAD JUST finished my second glass of merlot, considered getting another, then decided not to. I pulled out my Eric Benet CD, placed it in the carousel, and pushed the play button. I had a telephone call to make and I didn't need to be high. I located my leather organizer and turned to the Ts. My eyes scanned down a couple of names and then came to Raymond Tyler.

I picked up the phone and dialed his number. Right before I punched in the last number I started to hang up, but as with the third glass of wine, I resisted. After a couple of rings I heard the voice that still caused my heart to beat a little faster. It had been over two years since I had spoken with the only one who ever made me think I could spend more than a night with another man.

"Hello."

"Raymond. How ya doing, guy?"

"Basil. Whassup, dude? I'm surprised to hear from you," Raymond said.

"So I can still surprise you. That's a good thing."

"I guess I shouldn't say I'm surprised. I really expected to hear from you sooner."

"Why is that?"

"I figured you guys would make a run at my little brother. He told me you were a part of some firm in New York."

"Yeah, I gave up the TV thing. I'm a biznessman now," I joked.

"I'm happy for you. So I guess you know my little brother is now a big-time NFL player," Raymond said proudly.

"And he's kickin' ass. He's playing for San Diego, right?"

"Yeah. So why didn't you guys come after him?"

"'Cause we heard he was going with the big white firm in Chicago," I said.

"That's not true. My pops wasn't going to let that happen," Raymond said.

"Who did he sign with?"

"Carl Poston out of Houston."

"Is he happy with him?"

"Yes sir."

"Good. We brothers have to look out for each other and the Poston Brothers are some of the best in the business," I said.

"So, if you didn't call me about my little brother, then what can I do for you? You're not in trouble, are you?"

Suddenly I got a little nervous and wasn't ready to ask Raymond to be in my wedding, so I moved the conversation in another direction.

"So how's your boy?"

"I don't know how many times I have to tell you this, but his name is Trent and he's doing fine. How's your boy?"

"What boy?"

"I know you, and you got somebody keeping you warm in cold-ass New York."

"I do, but it's not a boy. I'm not swinging that way anymore."

"You're kidding, right? So you moved to older men?"

Raymond's last comment pissed me off and I started to let him know, but I remained calm and said, "I'm in love with a beautiful young lady and I'm getting married in a couple of months."

"So I guess congratulations are in order. I don't know what's going on, but there must be something in the air," Raymond said.

"What are you talking about?"

"You're the second person I know this year who's changed the way they swing. I mean, I remember when AIDS came out a lot of dudes started getting married, and it looks like the second wave is occurring."

"I don't know about that. All I know is that I'm in love and this is the right thing for me," I said confidently.

"Are you sure?"

"Very sure."

"Then I'm happy for you. Send me an invitation and I'll send you guys a toaster or something."

"Well, I was hoping for something more," I said as my stomach started doing somersaults.

"What is that? Help to arrange that last boy fling?" Raymond asked with a *boy I'm having fun fucking with you* tone in his voice.

I took a deep breath and then in a rushed tone of voice I asked, "Will you be in my wedding?"

There was a brief silence that seemed more like an hour, then Raymond finally said, "You're kidding, right?"

"No, I'm not kidding," I said firmly.

"Basil, man, we've been through this before. Remember when you were going to marry the young lady who you made love to while I slept in your closet?"

"What's your point?"

"You asked me to be in that wedding, which didn't take place," Raymond said.

"Man, that was years ago. I had forgotten about that."

"I'll ask you what I asked you then. Why would you want to have someone you once shared an intimate relationship with looking over you while you make a big mistake?"

"This isn't a big mistake. So you think what we had was intimate?"

"Don't you?"

"Dude, I didn't call to talk about us. I just wanted to ask you to be a part of the most important day of my life," I said, suddenly wishing I'd had that third glass of wine.

"Basil, listen to me. I'm honored that you would ask me to be a part of your big day. But I don't think it's such a good idea. I don't think it's fair to you or your new bride. And man, when are you going to free yourself?"

"Free myself—what are you talking about?"

"Does your bride-to-be know about your other life?"

"My other life?"

"Let me put it this way. Does she know about me or the other guys you've shared—how shall I say this—the men you shared special moments with?"

"That was the past. I love her and she doesn't need to know."

"Basil, as long as you have secrets you'll never be free."

"Raymond, I didn't call you for a lecture about my sexual life and freedom. If you don't want to be in my wedding, just say, 'Hell no,'" I said with an adrenaline-charged voice. I pictured Raymond with a cocky grin on his face. I could feel a thin glaze of perspiration forming on the back of my neck.

"It's not that I don't want to. I just know I shouldn't. But I wish you nothing but the best. We all deserve to be happy and free," Raymond said.

I was so mad I wanted to throw the fucking phone in my fireplace, but I said, "Thanks for reminding me how much you gay mofos piss me off!"

3 6

IT WAS the last week in November and the last week for Yancey's Vegas stint. Darla and Yancey were walking to the Luxor Hotel for a late supper, enjoying the moon, whose orange sorbet glow seemed to hang over the city. Even though it was late, the air was thick and hot, like a steam bath. Darla had invited Yancey to dinner to talk more about the wedding and promised the best mango margaritas in town.

"Did you see the new guy who just joined the show tonight?" Darla asked.

"The cute Italian guy with that tight body?" Yancey asked.

"Yeah, he's the real deal," Darla giggled.

"You sure he's not one of those *looks like Tarzan but acts like Jane* guys?"

"Maybe, maybe not. But I tell you what, if he's all

Tarzan, then I'd jump him for a nickel and give him some change back."

"You're so wild," Yancey said as they came to a stop-light. Darla made her smile and that was a welcome pleasure.

"I'm not playin'. Girl, it's been a while," Darla said as she moved her large leather bag from her left shoulder to her right shoulder. "I'm so sick of meeting *I'm waiting on a settlement* guys I don't know what to do. You know, the ones who are suing their former employer or some store where they slipped on some water. Trying to get rich the easy way. Vegas is full of them."

When the light turned green and the traffic sign flashed "Walk," the two started crossing. As soon as they reached the halfway point, Yancey turned to Darla and asked, "So are you going to be in my wedding?"

After a few uncomfortable seconds and right as their feet hit the curb, Darla looked at Yancey and said, "Sure. I don't know why, since we really don't know each other that well, but it sounds like fun. You don't need a flower girl, do you?"

"A flower girl?" She hadn't thought about a flower girl and assumed Ava would hire one.

"Yeah."

"I don't know, I need to check with my mother."

"Well, Mollie will be with me, and I know she would love to do it. Whenever I get a chance to include her with stuff I'm doing . . . well, it's a mother-daughter thing. When you have children of your own, you'll under-stand."

As they walked through the hotel's electronic double doors, Yancey gave her a half-amused smile and said, "I don't think so . . . about the children thing. But sure, Mollie can be in my wedding. We'd love to have her."

37

I WAS IN my office reading the sports section of *USA Today* when my assistant buzzed and told me Cavell Clemmons was on the line. I wasn't expecting to hear from that mofo anytime soon, especially since he still owed me money from bailing his ass out of jail.

I told her to put him through and I hit the speaker button on my phone, put my hands behind my head, and leaned back in my chair, prepared to hear a hard-luck story about my money.

"Mr. Clemmons," I said. "How in the hell are ya doing, sir?"

"I'm cool."

"Are you sure?"

"Doing the best I can. I'm just trying to work some things out. But I called to tell you I got your money and I'm going to drop it in the mail."

"Don't do that. I'll send over a messenger."

"What, don't you trust the good ole U.S. mail system?"

I started to say it wasn't the U.S. mail, but a former client who hadn't called since he left jail and got into a cab with the woman he was caught cheating with. When I got ole dude released I thought he might want to get a decent meal, but he and his lady friend vanished like ghosts once he sniffed the air of freedom.

"No, it's just easier. When we finish talking, I'll have Kendra get an address."

"Cool."

"So whassup with you and the Mrs.?"

"My soon to be ex."

"So you're going to be single again, huh?"

"Yeah, dude, and this time I'm going to protect my freedom like I protect my family jewels," Cavell joked.

"I hear you, dude."

"What is this I hear about you getting ready to give yours up?"

"Where did you hear that?"

"Man, I heard you are marrying some Broadway babe. My lady, not the wife, said she read it in some gossip column or some shit."

"Yeah, I guess so."

"You don't sound too sure, my brother. Learn from a brotha's mistake."

I told Cavell I was cool, but the mention of my upcoming marriage got me to thinking about Yancey and Derrick again. What surprise did he deliver? I was pretty sure dude hadn't come all the way to Las Vegas after five years to tell Yancey about some sick sister I had never heard her mention. I wasn't buying that, nor was I prepared to stop trusting Yancey based on one muffled conversation and some flowers. Still, I had had enough surprises in my lifetime from people who loved me. That's when the *bing* went off in my head.

"Cavell, let me ask you something about your previous situation."

"Ask away."

"You couldn't tell you were being taped? I mean, I thought there was some little beep when phone calls are being recorded."

"Dude, I told you, she bought some phones from this place called the Spy Store and they looked like regular phones. I didn't think nothing of it when I came home one day, and my wife was so excited about the new phones she had bought. I mean, she was always replacing shit in our house."

"So the phones look like real phones?"

"Dude, look like some shit you can buy right at the AT&T phone center," Cavell said.

"Man, that's some wild shit," I mumbled as I scribbled down "Spy Store" on a pad.

"You got somebody you want to record, Basil?"

"Maybe."

"I can find out where my ex bought the shit and the model number, dude. My lawyer got the information when we did the deposition on my upcoming divorce. He asked her where she bought the phones, how much they cost, and everything."

"Will you do that for me?"

"Sure, you need to help a brotha out every once in a

while. I'll get on it right now, and try to include it with the check."

"I appreciate that, Cavell."

"No problem. Us brothas got to look out for one another when it comes to them versus us."

"I feel you," I said. I drew a circle around the words "Spy Store" and then dotted it as if I had just hit the bull's-eye.

CAVELL PROVED to be a man of his word and I received the check and information on the phones. Kendra located a store near the office that had the phones in stock. I told Kendra I wanted to start taping my phone calls at home, just in case we ever ran into problems with clients and the NCAA. When I got to the store the salesman convinced me to buy a new device that was small and not as obvious as the spy phones Cavell's wife had used. It was the size of a microrecorder but could record up to a week of conversations.

The last couple of times I've talked to Yancey she's seemed troubled. Like there's something she wants to tell me but can't. The phone will tell me what's really on her mind. I hope it's only because she's getting nervous about starting a new life with me, but I've got to be certain.

I don't know what I'm going to do if Yancey is cheating on me. But I have to know everything possible about the woman I'm going to spend the rest of my life with. The woman who will bear my children. I told myself that was my reason when I paid cash for a recording device that I could attach to Yancey's phone. I told myself again when I attached it to her bedroom phone, right next to my picture.

My plan was going off without a hitch until I was on my way out of Yancey's townhouse. Windsor walked out of the kitchen with a sandwich, potato chips, and a glass of soda. We both surprised each other and, after a few uncomfortable seconds, I told her I had planned a surprise for Yancey's return. She looked at me and smiled, and then in typically female fashion said, "You are the sweetest man I've met in a long time. Yancey is very lucky."

"Thank you. I'm really looking forward to having Yancey back in New York," I said.

"You must be excited about the wedding as well," Windsor said as she set the plate on the bar and put a chip in her mouth.

"Yeah, I am. You will be there, won't you?"

"Of course. Even though I was a little too hefty to be in the actual wedding party, I'm going to offer to help out any way I can," Windsor said.

I looked at her closely to see if there was any sadness in her eyes. Yancey had told me it was Windsor who didn't want to be in the wedding. She said nothing about Windsor's weight, which didn't look that bad to me. I thought about what a nice lady she seemed to be, teaching and doing so much volunteer work at Hale House.

"Windsor, are the people at Hale House going to send the receipt directly to my office or my home?"

Windsor was drinking some of her soda but her eyebrows arched and she asked, "What receipt?"

"The one for the donation I gave a couple of months ago."

"Who did you give it to?" Windsor asked.

"Yancey. Didn't she give you a check?"

"Yeah, but she didn't say it was from you," Windsor said. "A couple of months ago she gave me a check for fifteen hundred, but I assumed it was her personal donation. Do you want me to check with her?"

"Naw, I probably misunderstood her. Maybe it was for some other charity," I said. Yancey had lied, and now any feeling of regret I had about spying on her was quickly replaced by a sense of duty. I didn't like anyone playing with my heart—or money.

"I hope I haven't said anything wrong," Windsor said. She gazed at me thoughtfully.

"No, Windsor, you haven't said anything wrong. Look, I'm getting ready to bounce out of here. Now, remember to keep my little surprise a secret. I want to see how long it takes Yancey to discover it."

"No problem. Your secret is safe with me."

39

YANCEY WALKED through the automatic doors at the airport and smiled to herself at the thought of being back in New York City. The gust of wind felt cold and refreshing, a welcome change from the heat of Las Vegas. The coolness caressed her face like Basil's strong hands. She pulled a floral silk scarf from her bag and wrapped it around her neck, thinking she couldn't take any chances with allowing the change in temperature to affect her voice. She had to be careful, especially since Lois had promised lots of auditions, mainly because of the rave reviews Yancey had received in Vegas.

She moved swiftly across the walkway and noticed an overweight African American man holding a sign with her name on it. Yancey walked right up to the car and, without a word, the driver opened the back door. In fact, Yancey didn't say a word until she was standing at her front door and murmured, "This is for you," as she placed a folded ten-dollar bill in the man's hand.

"You have a nice day, miss," he said as he politely tipped his hat.

Yancey had a busy afternoon planned on her first day back home. First stop after dropping off her luggage was a hair appointment at Scissors New York, the favorite salon of Broadway's divas. Then she had an appointment for a massage, and was ending her day by trying on wedding gowns at a tony dress shop on Fifth Avenue that Ava had located during her visit. Ava had wanted to pick out the gown herself, but when Yancey had been firm with her denial, Ava had sent beautiful four-color photos of gowns and possible bridesmaid's dresses. Yancey had to admit that the dresses looked beautiful, and she was grateful for Ava's scout work since she was short on time with the wedding less than a month away.

YANCEY was savoring the last sip of her wine as it ribboned down her throat. She was inspecting her wedding invitations, which had been sitting on her desk when she arrived home from her successful day of errands. She moved her hands across the thick, cream-colored cards with her and Basil's names embossed in gold lettering. She picked up a matching envelope lined in gold foil and thought how absolutely beautiful they were. The only problem she had was that Ava's full name was on the top line, but that was okay, since Ava had offered to pay for everything. Yancey studied the names closely to make sure Ava's full name wasn't bigger than hers. She then admired the picture of the beautiful ivory tulle and lace gown she had picked.

The house was quiet and Yancey was relieved it was Windsor's night at Hale House. She was on her way to the kitchen for another glass of wine when the phone rang. She figured it was Basil calling to make sure she had arrived home safely.

"Hello."

"Yancey." It was Ava, clear as crystal, without the echo and static of her cell phone.

"Oh, I'm so glad you called. I found the most beautiful dress, and the invitations arrived. Thank you so much for ordering them. I'm getting so excited. And you were right, the shop on Fifth Avenue was just wonderful," Yancey said.

"Are you sitting down?" Ava asked flatly.

"No."

"I think you better. I got some news that might make you cancel your wedding."

Yancey lowered her body down slowly to the bed, wondering what Ava was talking about. Had her newest husband left her with his money in tow? So now she couldn't afford the dream wedding she had promised Yancey.

"What are you talking about?" Yancey asked as she set the empty wineglass on the nightstand.

"I just got back some information from the detective I hired," Ava said.

"Okay. Is Basil not as wealthy as we thought?"

"No, it's not that. But he gave me some information that is a showstopper."

"What? Tell me," Yancey said as her voice suddenly went higher.

"Did you know he was seeing a shrink?"

"Is that what you're calling me about? Yes, I knew he saw a doctor to help him deal with the issues about his father not telling him about his mother. He told me about that when we met," Yancey said. Her heartbeat resumed its normal pace.

"Did he also tell you that he was a woman-hating bisexual with anger issues?" Ava asked.

"What are you talking about?" Yancey's heart began to race.

"I'm looking at it right here. My guy was able to get the information right from the doctor's office. I'm looking at the notes right now."

"How could you get doctor's notes?"

"When you got money and the right guy you can get anything. Trust me when I say that," Ava boasted. "The P.I. got the info from the lady who transcribes his notes."

"Are you sure the information is about Basil?"

"Yancey, I'm sorry, honey, but your husband-to-be admits to hating women, has an uncle who molested him, fell in love with some guy named Raymond . . . I mean, he doesn't like women at all. I'm surprised you haven't picked up on this. Most gay men I know like women. He talks about using a call-boy service for sex and how his career would have been ruined if anyone found out. Matter of fact, he even talks about killing his uncle."

"His uncle is dead," Yancey said.

"Well, you better check the death certificate and make sure he died of natural causes."

Yancey was silent for a moment, before an adrenaline rush of anger flooded her body as she thought of Basil sleeping with another man. Her lips parted in disbelief as her mind began to reel into a state of shock. Was he with men all the times he had said he was with Cade? Suddenly, a disturbing thought entered her mind and she screamed into the phone, "I bet that mutherfucker is fucking his nephew!"

"What are you talking about?"

"His nephew. I told you how attached he is to his sister's son."

"Yes, but there's nothing about him being a child molester," Ava said.

"But don't most children who are molested become molesters?" Yancey asked.

"I don't know, but I've read this report about five times."

"I still don't believe this," Yancey said as her eyes suddenly moved to a photograph of Basil sitting on her dresser. She picked it up and threw it across the room. Tears pooled in her eyes at the sound of the frame shattering.

"How are you feeling? I started to jump on a plane and tell you in person, but I figured you should know this as quickly as possible. Have you ever seen any signs?"

"What signs? Basil is one of the most manly men I've ever been with. There is no way, no how, he doesn't enjoy making love to me. If he doesn't, then Denzel got some competition in the acting department. Basil loves pussy!"

"Did you hear what I said? He's bisexual, and he might enjoy sex with you, but what if this Raymond guy comes back in his life . . . you could be there looking like a fool. I say cut your losses and move on."

Again Yancey became silent, and then she said, "Maybe this is a sign."

"What are you talking about?"

"Maybe this is a way of somebody telling me I need to marry Derrick and be a mother to my child." Her voice wavered between disappointment and fear.

"Are you crazy? I thought you told Derrick no deal. And we don't have to do any kind of investigation to know he will never make the kind of money to provide you with the life you deserve."

"Maybe I don't deserve to live a good life," Yancey said.

"Stop talking like that! Of course you deserve a fabulous life, and I'm going to make sure this mutherfucker makes a huge down payment toward that life."

40

WITH YANCEY back in New York, I decided to leave. I wanted to give her enough time to reveal her true self. She didn't seem to mind when I told her I had to leave for Florida on the day she returned from Las Vegas. I wasn't exactly lying. I needed to check on some players we were after in Gainesville and I stopped to spend a couple of days with my dad.

Even though I blamed my dad for a lot of the things that happened in my childhood, I still respected the way he managed to raise me almost single-handedly. Do I wish there were some things he would have done differently? Yes. But I now realize he made what he thought was the best decision regarding my mother. I also know he wasn't totally responsible for what my uncle did to me.

When I arrived in Jacksonville my dad was happy to see me. Even though I spoke to him regularly, my visits had become more infrequent. I had a wonderful time with him. We went fishing, drank beer, and caught up on each other's lives.

My last night he barbecued, and we started talking about women. He was between women but had several prospects. When he told me he would be sure to bring a great-looking one to my wedding, I told him about some of the doubts I was starting to have about Yancey. He looked at me with his narrow face and big, widely spaced eyes and said, "Be very sure about this, son. Marry the wrong woman and you can ruin a whole lot of lives." I didn't answer because I didn't want my voice to give away the emotions I was feeling. I just looked at him, trying to force a brave smile. I left Jacksonville for Miami confident that whatever I decided my dad would support me two hundred percent.

I visited with a few players at my alma mater, the University of Miami, and then headed to Fisher Island for some more rest and reflection. I thought a lot about my love for Yancey. How it had become the type of love that rearranges your life and the way you viewed love, like it's the first time you realize love has power that could make strong men suddenly weak.

I spent a lot of time walking on the beach wondering if spying on someone was the way to start a marriage. The ocean seemed restless, like me, the sun hazy but hot. Did I really need to know everything? I realized there were certain things I kept from Yancey, like my past with men. How in the past I used beautiful women only to make me feel better about my manhood. Was I doing it again with Yancey or was this love different? But what secrets was Yancey keeping from me? When I spoke with her it was always brief; I didn't want to seem suspicious. I sent her flowers every other day and she seemed immersed in getting back into New York's frantic pace and preparing for the wedding.

The week ended with only more questions. I was getting on the plane for Washington, D.C., and smiled to myself at the thought of something Nico had said when we lost our first money-making client to a bigger agency. "Life is a bitch, my friend. Always wear boxing gloves and a metal jock."

YANCEY WOKE up with her mind made up. She picked up the phone next to her bed and dialed Ava's number.

"What do you want this early in the morning?" Ava asked when she picked up the phone. Yancey had forgotten the time difference.

"I'm sorry. Can you talk?"

"Sure, darling. Did you get that information I faxed you?" Ava asked. She was talking about the notes from Basil's doctor visits.

"Yeah, I spent half the night reading it over and over. Can you believe some of the shit he told his doctor? Like pussy being a truth serum. And love being for punks, suckers, and females? When I get through with John Basil Henderson, he's going to be sorry he ever licked my pussy."

"So do I call the people in New York and tell them to put a hold on our plans?"

"No, don't do that. Full steam ahead. I'm going to marry Mr. John Basil Henderson," Yancey said.

"Are you sure you still want to marry this jerk?" Ava asked.

"Yeah."

"But why? Are you that much in love?"

"I didn't say I was so in love. I just have a plan."

"Oh, this sounds wicked. Talk to me."

"I plan to marry Basil and let him hang himself. Surely he's going to slip. All men who think with their dick do. And then I'll divorce his ass so quick that he'll think he's been punched out by Evander Holyfield," Yancey said. "He'll be seeing stars."

"Looks like I taught you well," Ava giggled.

"I'm going to make Robin Givens look like Mother Teresa. If he doesn't give me half of what he's worth then I'm going straight to the press. You don't know how badly he wants into the Pro Football Hall of Fame, and this will certainly stop that train."

"You're so right. And he hasn't brought up any prenup shit, has he?"

"No, and he better not or I'll reveal his secret before the wedding."

"Oh, this is going to be so much fun. You know, we should get the guy I hired to start following him right now. I bet he's going to hook up with his boyfriend before the wedding," Ava said.

"Yeah, maybe we can catch him in the act. Film at

ten!" Yancey's laugh floated in the room like a hot-air balloon.

"You read in the report where one of his girlfriends caught him. Aren't we lucky she kept her mouth shut?"

"You got that right. This way I get to play the beautiful jilted wife whose macho husband got caught with another man. Everyone will feel so sorry for me and I'll be laughing all the way to the bank. Hollywood will make a movie about it."

"I hear you, but I've got a question for you."

"I'm listening."

"How are you going to avoid sleeping with him?"

"Why would I want to do that? I told you he's a fantastic fuck."

"Aren't you worried about HIV?"

"Ava, listen to you. We got the medical information. He's not HIV positive and we always use condoms. Besides, I plan to hook up a couple of commercials anyway, so I'll be busy. If not, I can always tell him I am on location or something. Since I won't be around it'll just give him more chances to get busted."

"Yancey, sounds like you have this under control, but be careful. He really sounds like a sick one."

"You know me, Ava. I'm like you. I'll survive."

4 2

I CHECKED INTO the Four Seasons hotel in George-town. When I handed the front desk clerk my credit card, she told me there was an urgent message from my office. I quickly called Kendra on my cell phone and she told me Yancey was looking for me. I wanted to go to the gym for a quick workout but I decided to call Yancey first. She picked up after only one ring.

"Hey, baby, you miss me?" I said.

"Of course I miss you. I couldn't remember where you were going when you left Fisher Island. Do you miss me?"

"Now, you know I miss you."

"Tell me how much," Yancey pleaded.

"I don't know if I'm lovin' you 'cause I'm missin' you or if I'm missin' you 'cause I'm lovin' you."

"Oh, that sounds so sweet. How long are you going to be in D.C.?"

"Well, I've got a couple of Howard players I need to see, and I got to get my monkey suit fitted," I said.

"I can't wait to walk down the aisle and see you standing there looking so good," Yancey said. "Who's doing your tux?"

"Everett Hall, this brother who does suits for some of the biggest stars in the NBA and NFL," I said.

"I can't wait to see it and I can't wait for you to see my gown," Yancey said.

"In two weeks."

"Two weeks," Yancey repeated.

"Yep! Two weeks from Sunday I will be all yours," I said.

"Forever and always?" Yancey asked.

"And you know it. But I need to warn you: The next couple of weeks are going to be brutal," I said.

"How so?"

"It's coming up on Christmas and the bowl season and all my top players expect to see me at some of their practices. Especially those going to the Sugar and Rose bowls. Since we'll be on our honeymoon, I need to explain to them why I won't be at their games," I said.

"I hope they won't get mad."

"Don't worry. I can handle my young pups. All I have to do is show them a picture of the beauty I'm marrying," I said.

"You're going to make me cry."

"I don't want to do that, so let me get to the gym," I said.

"I love you," Yancey said sweetly.

"And I love you back," Basil said as the words caught slightly in his throat.

I T WAS a little before ten o'clock when Yancey awoke. The morning was clear and cool, with thin clouds streaking the sky. The house was quiet as Yancey moved from her bed's frigid sheets and went into the bathroom. She brushed her teeth and then washed her face with imported lavender soap.

She returned to her bedroom and sat near the head of her bed. As she looked at the phone and the remote control, Yancey was thinking about Derrick and Madison, trying to decide whether or not she should call, or avoid calling by watching television. She picked up the remote control and pressed the button, and suddenly she was looking at Rosie O'Donnell.

The night before she had dreamed about Derrick and Basil. They were asking her to choose and they were both holding children. Derrick with a little girl. Basil was holding a little boy. Yancey had turned and run down a dark alley with the children crying, "Mommy, please come back."

The phone rang and Yancey put the television on "mute."

"Hello."

"Yancey."

"Derrick?" Her voice sounded genuinely shocked.

"How are you doing?"

"I'm doing well. This is so strange. I was just thinking about you," Yancey said softly.

"Were you thinking good thoughts?"

"Derrick."

"Okay, I won't go there. I wanted to give you a little time to think about everything. But my sister is getting close to crossing over and I just wanted you to know," Derrick said.

"I'm sorry to hear that. How is your family holding up?" She wanted to ask how Madison was handling things, but she still couldn't say her name.

"Oh, we're a strong family, and right now all we're trying to do is be supportive, being there for Jennifer and making sure Madison is fine."

"That's good," Yancey said softly. For a moment she wondered what Madison looked like. Did she favor Derrick? Herself? Or was she a combination of her parents?

"So, have you thought any more about my offer?"

"Your offer?"

"Yeah, about becoming a part of our lives."

"How does your sister feel about this?"

"Jen wants what's best for Madison and me. That's

what's important to her. She was happy when I told her about seeing you and telling you about Madison."

"Derrick, I've still got a couple of things to work out. If you need money or anything, I will be in the position to help you at the beginning of the year," Yancey said.

"Yancey, we don't want your money. We have a comfortable life," Derrick said.

"I didn't mean to offend you. I'm just trying to let you know I want to help."

"I understand. But I've told you what I want you to do. I just don't know if I can wait forever."

"Derrick, I need more time."

"How much time?"

"I don't know. Derrick, I'll call you soon," Yancey said. She hung up the phone without saying good-bye or saying her daughter's name.

YANCEY spent the next hour staring at a mute television. It did register at some point that Rosie had gone off and *The View* was now on. She thought the show might take her mind off Derrick and Madison, so she hit the "volume" button. A few minutes later the phone rang.

"Hello."

"Yancey! This is Lois. I've got some great news."

"What?" Yancey asked flatly.

"A couple of things. The producers of *Chicago* called and made an offer for you to star on Broadway for three months and then do the part in London."

"London? I don't want to go to London. I'm getting married," Yancey said.

"But this is a great opportunity! I'm sure after you do London there is a chance you can come back to Broadway again," Lois said.

"What part of 'I don't want to go to London' don't you understand? What's the other news?"

"I got a call from George Tillman's agent. You know, the guy who did *Soul Food*."

"Yeah?" This sounded better to Yancey.

"He's doing a new film and he wants you to read for the female lead. Cuba Gooding, Jr., and Robert De Niro are already signed up."

"That's wonderful! I love all three of those men," Yancey said. She stood up from her bed and moved her right hand through her hair.

"Well, you can thank the producers of *Chicago*," Lois said.

"How so?"

"It seems George Tillman's wife saw you doing *Chicago* in Vegas, and I'm pretty sure she told him about you."

"So I'll have to thank them, but I'm still not listening to what they are talking about. If they can't give me an extended run on Broadway, then I'm not interested. There have got to be some new shows coming up or workshops. It's time for me to get my Tony Award and I'm not going to get one taking over roles somebody else has already done. You do understand that, don't you?"

"I don't think you should make a rash decision. I'll call Mr. Tillman's people and set up a screen test and I'll keep my ears to the floor about workshops. How are the wedding plans coming?"

"Fine, I guess. My mother is handling everything."

"Aren't you lucky? I'm looking forward to meeting your mother."

"Don't worry. I'll make sure you meet her. I've got to run. It's time for me to get to the gym."

"Have fun. I'll call you when I have something set up. Have a great day."

"I will."

Before Yancey left for the gym she placed a call to Basil and left him a message saying she was thinking about him. No reason for him to notice a drop-off in her sweet messages because she knew he slept with men, she thought. She then called Ava to give her an update on her career and Derrick.

After a few minutes of Ava updating her on the wedding plans, Yancey told her about her earlier phone call.

"I think this is bordering on harassment," Ava said.

"What are you talking about?"

"Derrick calling you. You told him you'd call him once you made a decision. If you want me to take care of him, I will."

"I can take care of Derrick," Yancey said. God knows what Ava would do, and Yancey didn't have any money for bail.

"I hope you're not leading him on."

"I might be. Who knows? I might be looking for a new husband next year." Yancey laughed, trying to put some humor in the conversation.

"I hope after you get out of this marriage coming up, you'll just take some time and enjoy your newfound wealth. You don't need a husband to do that."

"You got that right. Basil called me last night and I sweet-talked him just the same."

"That's a smart thing to do. I guess I taught you well." Ava laughed.

"To borrow a phrase from the B-boys, True dat," Yancey replied.

4 4

I TOOK THE train back from Washington, D.C., and was greeted by a rainstorm. I got in a cab and called Yancey. No answer. I figured this was as good a time as any to pick up the tape and see what my bride-to-be was up to. When I reached the apartment, I rang the bell to make sure Yancey or Windsor had not returned. After a few rings, I called her number again on my cell. Still no answer, so I took the key and entered. From the foyer I called out both Yancey's and Windsor's names. The house was silent.

I went into Yancey's bedroom and quickly removed the tiny recorder from under the table and the phone. My heart was beating faster, and I suddenly felt like Shaft.

When I arrived at my apartment, I looked through my mail, had a beer, and changed into some jeans and a knit shirt. I sat the recorder on my coffee table, then reviewed the instructions on playback. Once I figured out how to get the tape in the secret compartment to play, I suddenly felt a little anxious. What would I hear and how would it affect my relationship with Yancey? I had no clue as to what I was in for.

The first couple of conversations were with Yancey's agent and a couple of people calling about bills. All the phone conversations were pretty boring until I got to a call between Yancey and her mother. I couldn't believe Yancey and her mother were checking into my finances and personal life. When I heard Ava telling Yancey in another call about my visits to the doctor, I stopped the tape and hit the table with my fist so hard that I hurt my hand and had to ice it down.

I turned the tape back on and heard an interesting conversation, with Ava doing most of the talking.

"Yancey, darling, I'm on top of the world."

"What happened?"

"Sister, I just had the best sex I've ever had."

"I thought you said your husband was below average in bed."

"He is. But Hector of overnight express isn't. He is the best fuck I've ever had."

"You slept with him?"

"There was no sleeping going on. We checked into a suite at the Beverly Hills Hilton and we fucked over every inch of the space. I feel like a new woman."

"Are you going to see him again?"

"Are you kidding? As fast and as often as I can."

"Ava, please be careful. Your husband might not be as lame as you think."

"I don't care. I've got to have that man again."

"Well, I know how good a roll in the sheets is. If Basil starts to slack up, then I might need to start sending myself some packages and see what I can drum up."

I was pacing back and forth wondering first what in the fuck was going on with Yancey and second, how I was going to sue the fuck out of that dumb-assed doctor I had trusted with my secrets. *How in the hell could something like this happen?* I thought as I went to the fridge for another beer. I walked back into the living room and turned the tape back on. I skipped over a couple of calls, and stopped when I heard a man's voice. It was Derrick. It sounded like Yancey was telling the truth about his sister being sick. But who was Madison? Then I came across a call that revealed what I was dealing with.

"When is that Darla child coming in?"

"A week before the wedding. She's trying to set up some meetings with agents. Even though I think that's going to be tough with her limited talent. And even though she has a good body, she's not that cute. Did I tell you what she told me about Nicole Springer?"

"Nicole Springer? I haven't heard that name in a while. What about her?"

"She has twins."

"I didn't think she could have kids."

"Well, she does. I guess I didn't put enough of that shit in her coffee to kill her. I heard she's going to be in that show Dottie as well."

"You should be in that too. And if we get another chance to get her ass, you let me know. This time I will make sure she spends more than a few days in bed."

I shook my head. I couldn't believe that Yancey and her

mother had tried to do someone major damage. That had
to be a mistake. Maybe I was hearing things, or they were
joking, even though their voices sounded dead serious.
Most of the times they were talking about wedding plans,
but then I came across a conversation that would have
destroyed a weak mofo's soul. *"I'm going to call Derrick
and ask him not to call me anymore. Even when his sister
passes."*

*"I'm so happy you're finally listening to me. There's noth-
ing you can do for Derrick and that child."*

*"Ava, stop referring to her as that child. Like it or not,
she's your granddaughter and one day we both are going to
have to deal with her."*

*"I'm nobody's grandmother. And you don't have to deal
with her unless you want to. How can I drive it into that
thick skull of yours that when you signed those papers giving that child up for adoption, your responsibility ended.
When you get married or when you divorce that sick man
you're marrying, you will have enough money to make sure
Derrick and that child never find you."*

"I am kinda curious how she looks."

"Why?"

*"I don't know. I've just been thinking about that a lot the
last couple of days. She will be the only child I ever have."*

*"That's a wise move. They won't do anything but get in
your way, and if you ever get married again, marry somebody
old who's already done the father thing. There are plenty of
old-ass men like that."*

*"I doubt if I'd ever marry again. Once is enough for hav-
ing babies and getting married."*

"You got that right. Is Basil still out of town?"

"Yeah. I'm glad. I don't want to have to be around his ly-ing ass until it's absolutely necessary. It's a good thing I'm a great actress 'cause I'm going to need it the next couple of weeks."

"He doesn't need to know what we know until you're ready to take the money and run."

"What if he refuses to give me half?"

"You're holding all the cards, sweetheart. How many times have you told me how important that Football Hall of Fame is to him? All you got to do is threaten to spill the beans about Mr. Henderson's sex life. Maybe we can find that Raymond guy. There's no way he's going to get any Hall of Fame nothing if this shit reaches the press."

"I know you're right. He'll write me a check so fast the ink won't be dry by the time I get to the bank."

"He better. I'm investing a lot in this make-believe wed-ding. I expect big returns on my investment."

"Don't worry. You'll see a nice little profit. I promise."

"I believe you, darling. I've got to run. It's way early in the morning. This wedding takes up most of my day. I still got a husband I need to keep in the fold."

"You do that. I'll talk with you later."

I hit the "stop" button and felt my head swimming. I started to slam the machine to the floor, but there were still more recordings to listen to. I started shaking my head from side to side, asking myself how I could fall in love with a woman like Yancey. A woman who would turn her back on a child, then try and blackmail me. She had no clue who she was fucking with. I had to stop these crazy women before they destroyed not only my career but what was left of my heart.

I had become comfortable in the sulky silence of my apartment. I was trying to decide what to do next when my phone rang. *Who is calling me this late,* I thought as I moved from the sofa and looked at the caller ID, which displayed *"Out of Area."* I didn't feel like talking to anyone, but for some reason I hit the "speaker" button and sat back on the sofa.

"Speak," I commanded.

"Basil." I recognized the voice immediately. It was Raymond Tyler, number two on my list of mofos I didn't want to talk to.

"Raymond. Whassup? Are you calling to tell me again how worthless and wrong I am?"

"Naw, man. You've just been on my mind lately, and I called to apologize."

"Apologize? For what?"

"I was pretty hard on you when you asked me to be in your wedding. I don't know what got into me. If you've found someone who makes you happy, then I'm happy for you," Raymond said.

"So you calling to say you want to be in my wedding?" I asked. I slipped off my loafers and started to remove my socks.

"No. I still don't think that's a wise move, but I will try and make the wedding if you invite me."

"Don't worry. I don't need you in my wedding 'cause there ain't gonna be one," I said.

"Why not?"

"Man, females ain't shit, men ain't shit. The whole world is filled with a lot of sick mutherfuckers who just keep passing the hurt on from generation to generation.

That's why niggahs ain't ever gonna get nowhere. We just keep hurtin' each other."

"What's the matter, Basil? You sound really sad."

"No shit, Mr. Tibbs."

"What happened? Why aren't you getting married?"

I didn't answer Raymond immediately, partly because I didn't know if I was getting married or not. I stood up and unbuckled my pants and let them drop to the floor.

"Basil? Are you still there?" Raymond's voice was filling my apartment just like Yancey's and her mother's had earlier. But I could talk back to Raymond and tell him what I was feeling.

"Yeah, I'm still here," I said as I pulled my shirt over my head. There I was, standing in a dark apartment, stripped down to my black boxer briefs.

"Man, I don't know whassup, but I'm here if you need me."

"Are you really?"

"Yeah."

"You gonna be there if I end up blowin' some mofos up?" My words were weak-sounding, without conviction. I was mad, but I wasn't about to kill nobody and have to spend the rest of my life behind bars. Yancey wasn't worth that.

"You're not going to do that," Raymond said firmly.

"So you think you know me, huh?"

"I know you're not going to kill anybody. Do you want to talk about what's got you so upset?"

Raymond's question sounded just like a lawyer's. *Maybe he can help me,* I thought.

"How much time you got?" I asked.

"As much time as you need," Raymond responded.

"Hold on for a minute or two," I said as I went to the kitchen and pulled out another beer. I took a couple of long swigs before I walked back into the living room. I turned on a lamp and sat the beer bottle on the coffee table directly in front of the sofa.

"Are you still there, Mr. Tyler?"

"I'm still here."

For the next half hour I told Raymond my sad, sick love story. He didn't say much and when he did, I could tell he was choosing his words carefully. His elegant, deep voice was comforting and made me feel safe exposing something so embarrassing. I had to admit that one of the things I liked about Raymond was his sensitivity, something I wished I could express with someone besides Campbell and Cade.

"So what should I do?" I finally asked.

"Where do you want to start?"

"What about my doctor? Can I sue him for allowing the information to get out?"

Raymond said, "You know us modern-day black folks. We don't march anymore. We sue."

"Come on, be serious," I said.

"You could, but you wouldn't win if he could prove he had nothing to do with the information getting out, which it sounds like he didn't. You might have a case against whoever in his office with the lack of ethics, but you probably won't get any money."

"I don't want any money. I got my own money. I just want somebody to pay."

"You want to know what I think you should really do?"

"What?"

"Move on. I know it might not be easy, especially if you still love this lady, who sounds like she has a lot of problems of her own. But remember what you said earlier about us hurting each other?"

"Yeah."

"Well, you have a chance to stop the hurt in your own life right now."

"How do I do that?"

"I know this might be difficult, because it was for me, but you can't lead the rest of your life with secrets that can destroy everything you've achieved and worked for."

"So what are you saying? That I should tell the world I've slept with men and women? You sound like somebody else I know." Raymond and Zurich must be cut from the same jock, I thought.

"That's not what I'm saying. But you were saying how this young lady was going to spill the information to the press if you cancel this wedding so close to the date, and how that might hurt your chances for the Hall of Fame, right?"

"That's what she said."

"So what are you going to do? Deny it?"

"Sounds like a plan to me. Can't nobody prove it unless they got some videotape. I'm freaky but I ain't into recording it. Besides, Yancey's got some secrets as well. Some shit she doesn't want her adoring public to know."

"So you guys are going to settle your differences in the papers? Keep slinging the dirt and the hurt?"

I was thinking about the questions Raymond was asking, trying to come up with a plan where I could still hold on to some of my dreams. Like having Campbell, Cade, and my father sitting in the audience proudly when I was inducted in the Pro Football Hall of Fame. That wasn't going to happen if it was up to Yancey and Ava. I still wanted children of my own, but what if my past kept getting in the way?

"Is that what you want to do?" Raymond asked. His voice brought me out of my trance of questions.

"I don't know what I want," I said sadly.

"Let me ask you something we've been avoiding."

Well, here it comes, I thought. *Raymond is getting ready to ask me if I'm still attracted to men. He's going to say something silly and gay like "Pick a lane and stay in it."*

"What's that?" I asked.

"Do you still love, I'm sorry, what's her name?"

"Yancey," I said softly.

"Do you still love Yancey?"

"I don't know. How could I love someone who would try to hurt me?"

"Basil, at some point in life we all love someone who hurts us. It's one of the unfair things about life. But I'll tell you this, somehow we survive. And true love will come."

"Are you sure?"

"It's one of the reasons I still get up every morning. When you have love in your life it makes everything just a little bit better."

In the stretch of silence between us, I picked up my now warm beer and pulled it close to my lips. "Thanks, Raymond. I won't forget this."

45

I T WAS a week before the wedding and everything was going according to plan. Ava had come into town right before Christmas to make sure the hotel and hall were ready for what she was calling the last major social event of the millennium.

Later that evening Yancey was sitting on her sofa reading the script for the George Tillman movie. She had been expecting a call all day from Lois with information about the place and time of her audition.

Ava walked in carrying several shopping bags and floating as if she were among the clouds. Her mocha face looked pleased and excited.

"Where have you been?" Yancey asked.

"Taking care of business." Ava dropped her bags and took off her sable coat.

"I was worried about you."

"Why? I'm a big girl." Ava laughed.

"I know, but you didn't leave a note or anything. I came out of my shower thinking we were going to lunch and you were nowhere to be found. Windsor said you got a phone call and dashed out of here like a bat out of hell."

"That girl needs to mind her own business," Ava said.

"So where did you go?"

"Oh, here and there." Ava fussed with the packages.

"Spending more money."

"Look, I have something for you."

"What?"

"I hope you like these," Ava said as she handed Yancey an aqua Tiffany's box.

"Ava, what is this?" Yancey took the box.

"Open it."

Yancey removed the ribbon and opened the box to discover an Egyptian-style diamond-and-platinum tiara.

"Ooh, Ava, this is so beautiful."

"You like it? I thought it would be perfect for the wedding. I talked to the lady who's doing your wedding dress and she thought this would be great with the veil you're wearing. Let me put it on you to see how it looks."

Yancey turned her back toward Ava and released the ribbon in her hair and let it fall to her shoulders. Ava placed the tiara on her head.

"Go look at yourself. It looks stunning. You look like Miss America."

Yancey went over to the mirror and admired the gift from her mother.

"Ava, you shouldn't have done this. You're going to make me cry."

"Don't start getting soft on me," Ava said.

Yancey was touched and began to smile when the phone rang.

"You want me to get that?" Ava asked.

"No, that's alright. I'm expecting a call from Basil," Yancey said as she went over and picked up the phone. "Hello."

"Yancey?" It was Lois.

"Hey, Lois. I've been expecting your call."

"I want you to know I'm not a happy camper. What kind of games are you playing?"

"What are you talking about?" Yancey asked. Lois had never talked to her in such an annoyed tone.

"I just got a call from Mr. De Niro's agent."

"When is my audition?"

"You've had your audition," Lois said flatly.

"What are you talking about?"

"I called you today right before noon. Your mother said you were not available, but I told her that Mr. De Niro and Mr. Tillman were in town and wanted you to read. I told her how important it was and she promised to give you the information. The audition was set for two o'clock."

"I didn't get the message," Yancey said. She turned and looked at Ava, whose back was toward her.

"So is that why your mother showed up at the audition?"

"She did what?" Yancey asked, her voice soaring to a shout.

"She sure did. Told them that I had sent her and even had nerve enough to try and talk them into letting her read. The role is for a lady in her late twenties, not forties.

This is an embarrassment to me and my agency. I can't have this. It makes me look like a fool in front of two major Hollywood players. I think it's best that you and your mother find other representation immediately. Good luck with your career," Lois said. Before Yancey could respond she heard the dial tone.

She screamed out Ava's name so loud it startled both of them.

"What?"

"How could you do this to me?"

"Calm down, Yancey. I was just playing a little joke," Ava said as she waved her hand with a dismissive gesture.

"A little joke? You think my career is a joke?"

"I'm sorry. It was just when Lois called and told me you had an audition with Robert De Niro, well, something just came over me. I have been in love with him ever since I saw him in that movie with Sheryl Lee Ralph, *Mistress*. It was so good and he is so fine. Looks even better in person, and you know he has a weakness for black women. Who knows when I might be looking for another husband?"

Yancey was unable to speak or even look at Ava's face. She turned away to collect her thoughts, but then she whirled back around, her entire body shaking with rage.

"You're not upset with me, are you? I told them how great you were. I might have helped you get the part," Ava said with a slightly apologetic shrug.

"Get out of my house," Yancey demanded in a loud voice.

"What did you say?"

"I said get out of my house," Yancey repeated, pointing toward the door. Her eyes flooded instantly with tears.

"You can't talk to me like that."

"I'm not going to say it again. Get out of my house."

"You can't put me out of this house. My mother's money paid for this place, and I will go when I damn well please," Ava said. She sat down on the sofa and gave Yancey a look of pure contempt.

"Ava, please get out of here before I say something you don't want to hear."

"If you can dish it out then I can take it," Ava said as she stood up and moved closer until she was standing a few inches from Yancey.

"Do you know I don't have an agent now, thanks to you?"

"You said you were getting rid of her anyway. This just helps move the process along," Ava said nonchalantly.

Yancey's lips parted in disbelief as she asked, "Are you so insanely jealous of me that you are willing to ruin my career? Isn't it enough that you've ruined my life?"

"Jealous of you? Honey, the only thing I'm jealous of is the simple fact that you haven't let a lack of talent get in your way."

"You evil bitch," Yancey yelled, shoving Ava out of her way. Ava moved slightly to the left then hauled off and slapped Yancey so hard her ears rang.

"I should have done that a long time ago. Now you better pull yourself together 'cause you've got a wedding to get ready for," Ava said. She grabbed her bags and coat and darted out of the apartment.

• • •

ONE hour and two glasses of champagne later, Yancey was being swallowed by her own private heart of darkness. Her heart held too many painful memories, which had spilled over with the sting of Ava's hand. The lack of love Yancey received from her mother was like an open wound, but over the years she had developed a resolve so strong that she thought she could endure almost anything. Even a slap.

Yancey was lying on her back on the sofa, holding one of the pillows over her chest as if it were a treasured stuffed animal. The room was dimly lit with scented candles and a thin slice of light coming from the foyer bathroom. The phone rang constantly, but Yancey assumed it was Ava and finally unplugged it in the living room and kitchen. She was just about to get up and refresh her drink when she heard the key turn in the door. A few seconds later, Windsor walked in, turned on the foyer lights and then the living room lamp on the sofa table.

The lights startled Yancey. She sat up and screamed, "Turn out those damn lights!" Windsor didn't acknowledge Yancey's command. She was walking toward her bedroom when Yancey shouted again, "Didn't you hear me?"

Windsor turned around slowly and said, "I heard you the first time, Yancey, but before I answer you, why don't you answer a question for me."

Yancey, a puzzled look on her face, asked, "What?"

Without missing a beat, Windsor asked, "Why are you such a bitch?" She had indulged Yancey's evil diva behavior patiently during the time they had been roommates, but after spending the evening at Hale House, she was in no mood for an adult acting like a child.

"What did you say?" Yancey said, standing up.

"You heard me. Why are you such a bitch?"

"You can't talk to me like that. I'll kick you out onto the streets," Yancey said.

"My lease doesn't end until the fifteenth of January, remember? And if you try and kick me out, then I promise you'll regret it," Windsor said boldly.

Yancey was stunned to stillness, and her expression shifted from anger to surprise as she asked sarcastically, "I guess you just go in and out of that Jesus act, huh?"

"This isn't about me and my faith. This is about why you are so unhappy. You're getting married in a couple of days, you're famous, and I don't think you realize how blessed you are."

"You don't know nothing about my life."

"Then tell me, especially if it will explain why you're so unhappy."

Yancey was silent for a few minutes, and Windsor didn't move. When she started toward her room, Yancey asked, "Do you really want to know?" Her voice had softened.

"I'm here for you, Yancey. I've always offered you my friendship."

"I don't need friends, especially female friends."

"Why? So you can sit up here in the dark and feel sorry for yourself?"

"Because they've never liked me. They're always jealous of me, even my mother."

"I'm not jealous of you. Why do you think your mother envies you?" Windsor asked softly.

"She just does," Yancey said, tears beginning to flow down her cheeks. Windsor noticed the tears and moved close to Yancey to put her arms around her. The simple gesture was powerful, and Yancey started crying so hard that her chin was quivering.

"That's alright, get it out," Windsor said as she held Yancey tightly and gently brushed her hair with her hand. After a few minutes Yancey's crying stopped, and they sat quietly on the sofa. While wiping her eyes with an open hand, she told Windsor about Ava's afternoon escapade and betrayal. Her voice cracked as she said, "Ava has always been more concerned about herself. She has never been a mother to me, and now that her career is over she wants to ruin mine."

"Do you really believe that? Mothers just want what's best for their children. Just think about all the money she's spending on your wedding," Windsor said.

"Money means nothing to her. When she runs out, she goes out and finds another rich guy. I have spent my entire life feeling like I wasn't even good enough to be worthy of my mother's love. She always had a way of letting me know her career, friends, and husbands were more important than me," Yancey said, moving herself into a lotus position. For the next thirty minutes she told Windsor about the countless times during her childhood and young adult life when Ava had disappointed her. The hundreds of school plays Ava had promised to attend, but then only sent a card or a new dress. Windsor listened intently with intelligent eyes filled with both sorrow and concern.

"I have always tried to earn her love. I have done horrible things to people as a way of showing Ava I was like her, that I could deserve her love. But the only thing she's tried to offer me is friendship. I need a mother," Yancey cried.

"Have you tried telling her that?"

"She won't listen and maybe it's too late."

"It's never too late. You're getting married and it should be the happiest day of your life. You're going to need your mother with you."

"Don't even get me started on my wedding. Somehow I've let Ava mess this up for me as well," Yancey said.

"What are you talking about?"

Yancey told Windsor that Ava had discovered some terrible truths about Basil's past.

"But how do you know what she's telling you is true?"

"I know. Ava had proof."

"But Basil loves you."

"How do you know that?"

"I've been in love and I've been around love all my life. My parents are more in love today than when they first started dating, and that was over forty-five years ago. That look I see in my daddy's eyes, well, that's the look I've seen in Basil's eyes when I've been around you two."

"You really think so? I'm beginning to believe I can't trust anyone," Yancey said softly. Her eyes looked like they were pleading for a chance to explain all the pain they had seen.

Windsor took Yancey's hands and placed them in her own, then said, "You can trust me. I'm your friend."

"Are you really?" Yancey pleaded.

"Yes, Yancey, I'd love to be your friend. Everybody needs a friend."

"But I've been so mean to you."

"Now I understand why. We can forget about the past."

"So you'll be my first best friend?" Yancey asked, her eyes beginning to fill with tears once again.

"If you'll let me," Windsor said, and with her arms surrounded Yancey with a calming warmth that felt like magic.

46

AFTER LISTENING to Yancey's recording I spent a couple of days alone, away from the rest of the world. There were some things that made me particularly mad, like Yancey and Ava thinking they could run a game on me. There were some things that made me really sad, like Yancey assuming that I was probably molesting Cade. I would rather have her call me a cocksucker to my face on national television and then spit on me than have her say what she said.

I had to block her words out of my head. I spent most of my time listening to music and rearranging my CDs, underwear, and socks. I made a few calls to clients and some dudes I'm still looking to sign. I made copies of the Yancey recordings. I wasn't quite sure why I did that, but maybe they would come in handy later. I talked to Kendra about a trip I had scheduled to Wisconsin. At first I started to cancel the trip, but I figured work would take my mind off my problems. I spent an evening with Nico and Brison at Scores, an upscale tittie bar we sometimes took clients to. I didn't let them know my wedding wasn't going to happen. I behaved as if everything was the way it was supposed to be. Yancey the great actress called every day, but I managed to return the calls when I knew she wouldn't be available. I don't know what I would have done if I actually spoke with her, since I was still hotter than chicken grease.

I also spent a great deal of time painting possible scenarios in my mind about getting back at Yancey and Ava. I didn't come up with anything but I will, because the old Basil has returned. I needed a woman in my life like a dead man needs a casket. But I ain't never gonna be an *if loving you is wrong I don't wanna be right* kind of niggah.

IT was a dazzling winter evening in Chicago, with an endless blue sky dotted with clouds and stars. I had stopped in Chicago to celebrate signing another top player from the University of Wisconsin. Besides, I didn't feel any strong desire to be back in New York. I checked into a downtown hotel and called Zurich to see how he was doing with his solo business and to gloat about my new client.

We met for dinner at the Capital Grille, an upscale steakhouse right next to my hotel. Zurich had invited me to dinner at his home, telling me what a great cook his grandmother was, but I didn't want to spend the evening with the dude and his grandmother, no matter how good a cook she was.

Zurich and I both enjoyed an excellent piece of prime rib with baked potatoes and spinach. I had a couple of glasses of burgundy while Zurich had iced tea. We talked about the recent rash of pro football players getting in trouble over women, and about the upcoming bowl season. As we left the restaurant I turned to Zurich and asked, "Would you like to come up to my suite? I'm enjoying our conversation and there is something personal I'd like to talk with you about."

Zurich smiled and said, "Sure, I got a little time."

I think I invited Zurich over because I didn't want to do something stupid like calling an escort service for a little after-dinner piece of ass. I was, after all, a free man once again. It didn't matter that I hadn't told Yancey yet. I knew of a service in Chicago I had used once when I was doing games for ESPN. They had told me they had a really hot guy who was a dead ringer for Derek Jeter. I had gotten all excited, took a long bath, and put on some of my fancy silk draws. When the bell rang, I answered the door with my jimmie already rock-hard. But the dude standing at the door was so ugly, like a human Tweety Bird with yellow teeth, that it was as if somebody had massaged my jimmie with an ice cube. I didn't say shit to him as I slammed the door in his face. I was so mad I started to tip off the Chicago police about the agency, but changed my mind.

Zurich and I walked the long block to my hotel in silence, gazing at the Christmas trees, which looked as if they were winking at me and knew what I had on my mind. When we got back to the hotel he stepped back in a gracious manner and motioned for me to go through the revolving door first. It made me feel like he was treating me like a bitch, so I insisted that he go first and smiled at him playfully.

We walked into my suite and were greeted by gentle classical music. I offered Zurich a canned iced tea from the mini bar and excused myself to change clothes. I put on my nut-hugging black jeans with knife-blade creases, and a turtleneck the color of flaming coals.

I walked back into the living area barefoot and saw Zurich looking out of the large picture window.

"Chicago is a beautiful city, isn't it?" Zurich asked as he turned around with a smile full of teeth as white as a Caribbean cloud. Dressed in gray wool crepe pants and a white cotton oxford shirt, he was looking good.

"It's alright," I said, as I pulled a beer from the mini bar.

"Did I mention I was taking some classes at Northwestern's Law School?"

"Man, you're gonna have more degrees than a thermometer. Where do you find the time to run a business and go to school?"

"I go to bed early and I get up even earlier."

"Dude, I'd tip my hat to you, if I wore hats," I teased.

"So, what do you want to talk about?" Zurich asked.

His direct question caught me off-guard, so I tried to turn it back to him. "How's your love life?"

"That's what you want to talk to me about?"

"Naw. When is that article going to run? I've been looking for it."

"I don't know. One of the guys pulled out and threatened some legal action, even though my friend had the entire interview on tape."

"Are you still happy you did it?"

"Yeah, especially if it's going to help somebody." Zurich turned from the window to me and asked, "So when is the big wedding?"

"I don't want to talk about that," I said bluntly. A memory of Yancey came into my thoughts, but I quickly pushed it away.

"Whassup?"

"Dude, I said I don't want to talk about that."

"Then what do you want to talk to me about?"

"What if I just wanted to enjoy your company?"

"That's cool," Zurich said as he looked at his heavy silver watch.

"Your grandmother doesn't have you on curfew, does she?" I joked.

Zurich just shook his head and sat down on the sofa, so I sat down next to him. I was so close I could smell his masculine, sharp, citrus-scented cologne.

"So how is your friend?"

"What friend?"

"Your boy. The one who wrote the article."

"He's good, but I thought you wanted to talk about you."

Suddenly I really didn't know why I had invited Zurich to my room. Or did I? Was this my attempt to join his team again and get his tight body next to mine? Could Zurich be the one who could make me enjoy uninhibited sex with a man? Could he be my Raymond? I guess there was only one way to find out. I knew I couldn't count on Zurich to make the first move, no matter how bad he wanted to git with me.

"Excuse me one more time," I said.

"Sure, take your time." Zurich smiled. I noticed how easily he smiled and felt myself melting like butter on hot toast. Was this the kind of smile that came with being comfortable with yourself?

I went into the bedroom and pulled off my sweater, then dropped my jeans. I looked in the full-length mirror and noticed a glazed look of excitement in my eyes and my manhood stuffed inside the royal blue underwear, straining the silk-mesh fabric. I pulled my draws off and out plopped a fully erect jimmie. It was clear my jimmie was obeying no master but its own mind. Surely Zurich Robinson would recognize that I had a body that was meant for sex.

I stopped in the bathroom, brushed my teeth, put a little gel in my hair, and sprayed some cologne directly at the hairs on my chest. I took a close look at my soap-clean face and then winked at myself and said, "Let's do this!" I stood outside the bathroom door for a few uncomfortable seconds and then stepped confidently, and completely nude, into the living room.

Zurich was looking at a magazine, but when he looked up he jumped like he was afraid of snakes, especially the long and thick one I was carrying between my legs.

"Basil, what's going on, guy?"

"You tell me." I smiled slyly as I moved toward the mini bar and pulled out another beer. I could feel Zurich stealing glances at my ass, because when I turned around, his eyes weren't looking at mine. Suddenly a panicked irritation swept across his face, and he said, "I need to get home."

"Why you leaving, dude? The party is just getting started," I said as I sat on the sofa.

"Basil, why are you doing this? Is this your way of telling me you want to be with me?" His voice was low and husky, full of emotion. His eyes unreadable. There was a long, tense silence and my nude body suddenly was covered in a thin, nervous sweat.

I finally broke the silence to ask, "What if I did want to git with you? Are you game?"

More silence. Then Zurich started to speak very slowly, with pauses for me to speak, but I remained silent.

"Basil, I'm flattered . . . but . . . man . . . but I don't just hop in bed because some good—I mean great—looking man wants to. I . . . I . . . only make love with someone I'm intimate with. We don't have that. You're getting ready to get married. Why are you doing that when you're still attracted to men? Why cause this woman such pain and grief?"

"You don't know nothing about Yancey," I said. I started to tell him my wedding plans were off, but figured the less I said the better.

"Does she know that you're bisexual?"

"I don't want to talk about that part of my life. This is between you and me. If you don't want to git with me, that's cool. There are plenty of women and men that would love some of this dick," I said, suddenly feeling uncomfortable about being naked. I grabbed one of the small pillows on the sofa and placed it over my jewels. I wondered if Zurich was playing some type of game. Did he want me to rush him and just take the ass or did he want something more? I wasn't looking for a relationship. That would be a classic case of moving from Sodom to Gomorrah.

"Basil, I think you're a great guy, and if I wasn't trying to make things right with my friend, Sean, then I would definitely be interested in someone like you. But only if you're willing to be totally open and honest with yourself. I couldn't be involved with a man who might decide one day he wants a woman and will think it's alright. I want somebody who honors a relationship—no matter what kind of relationship. You got a slamming body, but I can't."

"Then leave," I said curtly. I shifted my body on the sofa.

"Are you going to be alright?"

I didn't answer, so Zurich repeated slowly, "Are you going to be alright?"

"I'm straight," I said and thought how ironic the popular saying felt at this moment.

Zurich stood up and started fumbling in his pockets. He pulled something from them and said, "I want to leave you with something."

"What?"

"This." He reached for my left hand and placed in it a gold ring with a burgundy stone.

"What is this?"

I noticed sweat glistening on his face, and when he spoke his voice took on a certain strength. "This is Milo's ring. Remember the young man I told you about? It has given me a lot of confidence and power to be able to look at myself in the mirror and be proud of the man I have become. I know that it doesn't matter to God or anyone else who I love. It's just important that I love. And when I say 'love' that includes sharing that love on a physical level, but not just because a handsome man greets me with an incredible erection. I want you to have this and believe that it will give you courage to make the right decisions about your life. You can be totally happy when you look at yourself in the mirror, even if there ever comes a time when you don't have a perfect body."

I gazed at the ring and then into Zurich's eyes, which had a look of promise and comfort. His thoughtfulness seemed sincere, but I couldn't speak as I closed my hand with the ring in my sweaty palm.

"Maybe one day you won't need the ring. Hopefully, when that day comes you will pass it on to someone who needs it. There will always be someone who will need it. Who knows? I might need it again. This life we live can be very cruel, but there will be many moments of joy."

My blank eyes roamed around the room in silence. The chilling emptiness and silence of the suite surrounded me.

"I'm going to leave now, but I'll call you in a couple of days," Zurich said. He walked out of the suite.

When Zurich left I turned out all of the lights. I felt lonely and rejected, and what pride I had felt earlier, nude and rock-hard, had vanished, but in the darkness it didn't seem to matter.

47

THE DAY before the big engagement party, Yancey and Windsor sat down in the kitchen to enjoy a midmorning breakfast and another conversation about Yancey's childhood. Yancey spent a day in solitude thinking about the fight with Ava and her wedding plans. The phone had rung almost every hour, but Yancey ignored it. She didn't want to talk with either Basil or Ava.

Yancey's and Windsor's plates were covered with pancakes that were slathered with butter and drenched in maple syrup, with steaklike portions of ham Windsor had prepared. This time when Windsor said grace, she took Yancey's hand and held it tightly. Yancey closed her eyes and listened to Windsor's words, which included a plea for God to ease Yancey's heavy heart and allow her to make the right decisions regarding her wedding plans. When Windsor finished, Yancey smiled at her and rubbed the top of her hand.

After a few bites of the soaked pancakes, Yancey picked up her mug and drank some of the gourmet coffee she had prepared. Her face seemed totally blank, and Windsor could tell she was still feeling troubled.

"Have you decided what you're going to do?" Windsor asked.

"Not yet. I still think I'm going to marry Basil so I can get my mother out of my life," Yancey said.

"Do you think that's the right thing to do?"

"I don't know," Yancey said. She placed the mug on the counter and added, "I've made such a mess of my life."

"But today is a new day, and you can start to heal right now," Windsor said.

"Can I tell you something, and you promise not to tell anyone?" Yancey asked. She had never shared deep, personal secrets with anyone but Ava.

"Sure, I can keep a secret."

Yancey took a deep breath and looked Windsor directly in the eyes before she said, "I have a child." She couldn't believe her ears when Windsor answered, "I know."

"How could you?" Yancey asked.

"I saw you the day you walked into Howard Hospital. I was doing volunteer work on the maternity ward taking care of babies who were being given up for adoption. Most of the time the mothers didn't want to see them after they were born and there can be lapses before the adoptive parents come. So, like I'm doing now at Hale House, I was holding the babies," Windsor said.

"Why didn't you say something to me?"

"I figured you didn't want to talk about it. I thought you might pick up on it when I told you I saw you once on campus and it looked like you had picked up some weight."

"Oh yes, I remember. Did you see my baby?" Yancey asked as she touched Windsor's hands.

"I don't know. I was leaving when you were coming in, and I didn't come back to the ward until a couple of days later and it was mostly newborns."

Yancey then told Windsor about Derrick's deception and about him offering Yancey a second chance to be a mother. She told Windsor how the days before and after the birth had been the worst in her life because she had finally accepted the fact that Derrick didn't really want to marry her and she was once again following her mother's path.

"Have you told Basil?"

"No, and I'm not going to. I can't ruin that little girl's life."

"Why do you think you'd ruin her life?"

"I've come from a long line of bad mothers. My grandmother, although she raised me, was resentful of me and my mother. Even though my grandmother wasn't out of the country working, Ava said she was never at home with her. Ava said she spent more time shacking up with some man and taking care of his kids than she ever did with Ava. Right around the time I was born, the man got back with his wife, and I guess it made my grandmother a very bitter woman. And Ava, there's not enough time in the day to tell you about all her exploits trying to deny motherhood. I was eight years old before she would even allow me to call her 'Mama.' Then it had to be only when we were alone. She wanted everyone to think we were sisters." Yancey felt a sudden sense of relief as she shared her family history. She was tired of making up stories of how wonderful her mother and grandmother were. Yancey had told so many lies that sometimes she didn't know what the truth was. As she talked, Yancey knew for certain she didn't want Madison's life ruined by her, Ava, and all the untruths.

"But Yancey, you're still young. You can change. There is nothing written that says you will be the kind of mother Ava was or wasn't. What are you going to do if Basil or whoever you settle down with wants children?"

"Then I'm not the one he should be married to," Yancey said firmly.

"You do want children, don't you?" Windsor asked.

Yancey was silent for a few minutes and then she looked at Windsor and asked, "Can I tell you something I've never shared with anyone?"

"Sure you can," Windsor said as she rubbed the top of Yancey's hand.

"I can't have children," Yancey said. "After I gave birth I had my tubes tied. I didn't want to risk having to make another decision like the one I made in that hospital room."

"But I think they can reverse that operation," Windsor said.

"Only if a person is willing. And I'm not willing, after everything I've been through, and I don't think there's a man in this universe who can make me change my mind," Yancey said.

Windsor just looked in sorrow at Yancey for about ten minutes. Just when she was getting ready to offer more words of understanding, Yancey started talking. She told Windsor how she wasn't allowed to have dolls or any toys when she was growing up. Yancey shared how her grandmother made her give away the dolls and some of the dresses Ava had sent from overseas because she didn't want her to be spoiled or think she was somebody special. If Ava sent two dresses, one had to be given away to Goodwill. Sometimes Yancey would see her classmates wearing dresses Ava had sent her. The memory of her grandmother's coldness caused tears to gather in the corners of her eyes, and Yancey fought to keep them from falling onto her cheeks.

Windsor pulled Yancey close to her breast and gave her a sisterly hug. The two gazed at each other in silence as Yancey wiped her face with the back of her hand, when they suddenly heard the sound of clicking heels on the hardwood floor in the living room. At first they were startled until they heard Ava's voice calling out Yancey's name. Yancey had forgotten she'd given Ava a key.

AVA walked into the kitchen draped in a different mink coat than the one she wore the day before and greeted them with a big smile and a question. "Is something wrong with your phone and am I too late for breakfast?"

"Good morning, Mrs. Middlebrooks," Windsor said. Yancey took another bite of her pancakes and rolled her eyes toward Ava.

"Good morning to you, Wyoming," Ava said as she moved toward Yancey and gave her a theatrical kiss on the cheeks. Yancey knew Ava was going to act as if the previous night had never happened and figured it would be best to join her mother's soap opera drama. But only after she had corrected her on the cast of characters.

"Her name is Windsor, Ava. Not Wyoming," Yancey said in a terse voice. Ava gave her a puzzled glare and Yancey returned it without backing off. "Oh, I'm sorry, Windsor. You know, sometimes I get a case of CRS, you know, *can't remember shit*." Ava laughed as she took off her coat and laid it over a bar stool.

"That's fine. I didn't take offense."

"Good. Yancey, I have some great news!"

"What?"

Before answering Yancey's question, Ava noticed the leftover pancakes and ham on Yancey's plate and said, "You didn't eat all that, did you? Honey, you better watch it or your little narrow hips are going to spread faster than a rumor." Ava spoke in the fake British accent she sometimes used, which always drove Yancey nutty.

Yancey ignored her comments and asked Ava about her big news.

"Guess who our publicist got to cover the wedding with an eight-page layout?"

"Who?"

"*In Style* magazine," Ava said as she clapped her hands with glee.

"That's so exciting, Yancey! My mother and daddy are not going to believe they are attending such a wedding. They are going to pass out when they hear about *Ebony* and *Jet* being there," Windsor said.

Ava rolled her eyes and turned to Windsor, then said, "Darling, can you excuse us for a few minutes?"

"Sure," Windsor said. "Just let me put these dishes in the sink." Windsor took both plates from the counter and scraped the leftovers into the garbage. She ran a little water over the plates, wiped her hands with a dish towel, and started out of the kitchen. When she got to the door, she looked at Yancey and said, "I'm here if you need me." Yancey gave her a grateful smile.

Ava waited a few moments to make sure Windsor wasn't lurking near the door. She even peeked out the door to make certain. She turned to face Yancey and asked, "What's going on here?"

"What are you talking about?" Yancey said as she refreshed her coffee.

"How is it that all of a sudden you two are Laverne and Shirley?" Ava asked nonchalantly, as if she were chewing bubble gum.

"Windsor's a nice girl. I decided I was going to stop being a bitch to her."

"Oh, I see. But you didn't tell me you were inviting her parents to the wedding. You might as well have invited the usher board from Jackson. I'm not planning some country wedding. You can't invite just anyone to your wedding, like it's some 'come one, come all' kinda evening."

"This is my wedding . . . right?"

"Yes, but it's my money."

"It's too late because I've already told Windsor they could come, especially since Windsor couldn't go home for Christmas because she has to move," Yancey said.

"That's not my problem. Besides, aren't her parents coming *here* for Christmas?"

"Yes."

"Well, I hope you didn't invite them to the rehearsal party, and we might want to hire somebody to keep an eye on them to make sure they don't talk to any of the reporters," Ava said as she looked into the cabinet and pulled down a dainty flower-covered coffee cup. She walked over to the coffeemaker and asked, "Is this still fresh?"

"Taste it," Yancey said.

Again, Ava rolled her eyes at Yancey in a suspicious manner as she sipped the black coffee.

"Where is that freak of a man you're going to marry?" Ava asked.

"I think he's spending some time with his sister and nephew."

"He hasn't asked you to sign anything, has he?"

"No."

"Great. Looks like we're home free," Ava said, placing the cup in the sink.

"I've been having second thoughts," Yancey said.

"Second thoughts about what?"

"This wedding."

"Cancel them. I've already spent too much money and somebody's getting married on Sunday. And since I'm already spoken for, it's got to be you," Ava said. She twirled her hand with a large diamond ring in front of Yancey. Ava reached for her coat and headed toward the door, but before she left, she turned to Yancey and said, "You don't look that good. Aren't you happy?"

"No, I'm not happy."

"Then you better act like it. You *are* still an actress, aren't you?" Ava snapped as she moved through the door.

LATE the same afternoon Yancey awoke from a jumpy nap with a thumping headache. She was getting out of her bed to get some aspirin when she heard Ava and Windsor talking in the living room. Yancey moved toward the bedroom door to lock it, but before she reached it Ava was standing in the room.

"Did you just wake up?" Ava asked.

Yancey, feeling totally defeated, nodded her head. She felt simply powerless to do anything but sleep.

"Girl, it's a good thing I'm running this show, 'cause if it was left up to you then nothing would happen. I got some more news."

"What?" Yancey asked. Tension stiffened her entire body.

"The fashion editor from *Ebony* called and they want to shoot you in your wedding dress the day before the wedding. I've already talked to the people at the shop and they will do a final fitting that morning."

"Why can't they just take the pictures at the wedding?"

"I don't know. I didn't ask them. We're just going to do as they ask."

"Whatever," Yancey mumbled as she moved to get the aspirin.

"I'm not going to tell you about your attitude one more time. And another thing, I don't want to spend Christmas with Windsor and her Beverly Hillbillies family. I have arranged for us to stay at a fabulous penthouse suite at the Peninsula Spa. We can do the final fitting, get facials and massages. Just like best friends. We will leave right after the party. That way I don't have to worry about you doing something stupid," Ava said with a condescending smirk.

"Now, what makes you think I would do anything to ruin this for you," Yancey said grimly, walking out of the room.

Ava started to follow her, but instead she shook her head in disgust.

FINALLY DECIDED to call Yancey. For the last couple of days I'd been avoiding her as if I were allergic, which is a polite way of saying I'm not certain I could control my emotions if I talked to her in person.

I hit the speed dial, then put the phone on speaker.

"Hello," Yancey said.

"You been thinking about me?" I asked.

"Where have you been? I haven't heard from you in a couple of days. I left you a couple of messages at home and your office. Is everything alright?" Yancey asked. There was a definite panic in her voice.

"I'm sorry, baby. I did get a couple of messages, but I've been working like a slave so everything will be in order for the big day and the honeymoon. I'm trying to make some more money so I can support you like the star you are," I lied.

"Do you love me? I love you," Yancey said. When I

heard her say "I love you" my entire body felt as if an electrical shock had surged through me. The words sounded flat and rehearsed. But I didn't react. I figured I had to go along with the game. But it was hard keeping Yancey and Ava's conversations from weaving through my thoughts. The knowledge that my secret lust wasn't a secret anymore made me ill. But this was no time to get sick. I had to get my payback.

"Of course I love you. Gonna spend the rest of my life with you," I said. "How are all the plans going?"

"Fine, I guess. Ava's in town and taking care of everything," Yancey said in the casual tone I was used to.

"Oh, that's great," I said. I wanted to ask what broom the Wicked Witch of the West had flown in on, but I resisted.

"Are you getting excited about the party tonight?" Yancey asked.

"The party?"

"Yeah, the engagement-rehearsal party at Laura Belle's. Ava says it's going to be wonderful."

"Oh yeah, I'm sorry. I've got a lot on my mind," I said. Zurich popped into my thoughts. I needed to call him and tell him I was sending the ring back. I didn't need anything to remind me of what a fool I had been when I was in Chicago.

THE ENGAGEMENT party of Yancey and Basil had more surprises than guests. Mostly from Madam Ava Parker Middlebrooks. Guests dined on smoked salmon and caviar on lemon toast, crab cakes, Cajun brochettes, and mushroom frittata. Ava spared none of her husband's money as she pulled out all the stops to show New York's elite and elite wannabes what a grand diva she was. In her mind, this wasn't about Yancey and Basil, but as always, it was about her.

Most of those attending the event could not say they personally knew Yancey or Basil, much less that they had ever heard of Ava. Throughout the evening, as guests were overpowered by the splendor of the imported flowers and ice-sculpted swans atop mirrored tables, they could be heard saying things like: "I don't really know Yancey, but I've seen her in a few shows"; "Yeah, back in the days when Basil was playing for the Warriors, I partied with him and a few of his teammates"; "I hear her mother used to be a big star in some part of the world."

About an hour into the party, the handsome couple danced in the center of the ballroom to Kenny Latimore's hit "For You." When Kenny's voice faded, Basil took Yancey's hand and led her off the floor. All kinds of thoughts were weaving through his mind. He thought of how beautiful Yancey looked, and for a second he wondered if he should have one more throw-down in the sheets. But when he remembered Ava telling him how happy she was to have him as a son-in-law, the reality of his doomed situation hit him like a body-slamming tackle.

"Are you okay?" Yancey asked.

"Why wouldn't I be? I mean, I'm on top of the world," he said.

"I thought you might be sad because your father didn't make the party."

"No, I'm fine. Besides, he will be here for the big day, and all he has to do is stand by my side," Basil said as he placed his hand at the small of her back. "Come on, let's go speak and introduce ourselves to some of our guests."

As Basil and Yancey drifted from table to table greeting their guests, Ava took to the bandstand and whispered to the conductor. She then took a fork and tapped her crystal champagne stem, asking for everyone to quiet down. A hush came over the room and all eyes fell upon Ava, dressed in a beige silk chiffon dress covered with colorful silk butterflies and flowers. She was also wearing a pink diamond and pink-gold heart necklace she had bought when she purchased Yancey's wedding tiara.

"First of all, I hope none of you were expecting a

chicken wing affair. Isn't the food great?" The ballroom suddenly filled with laughter. Ava continued, "I'd like to thank you all for coming out to celebrate the wedding of my beautiful daughter and her handsome, or should I say phine—spelled with a ph—future husband. As all of you know, talent runs in our family, so in a tribute to my daughter's gifts, I would like to serenade the couple with a few songs." Ava spoke in an unsteady voice, as one of the twelve tuxedo-dressed waiters refilled her glass for the eighth time. Ava took a swig of champagne, turned and looked at the conductor, and yelled, "Hit it, fellas."

Yancey and Basil were back at the head table, looking on in shock. Yancey was stunning in her formfitting light-green silk gown, the color of lettuce, designed by Anthony Mark Hankins. The dress had a plunging neckline and a small train sprinkled with exquisite beads and had guests wondering how she could possibly outdo herself for the wedding. A sable coat hung gently off her shoulders. Basil wore a silk crepe dark-gray suit, with a sky-blue shirt and matching tie.

Ava's first number was smooth and appropriate, "When I First Saw You," from the musical *Dreamgirls*. But the second number, a rendition of "And I Am Telling You," after another swig of her bubbly, was more Jennifer Lopez than Jennifer Holiday. Ava closed her set with a gut-bucket rendition of "I Got the Right to Sing the Blues," which she ended by kicking off one of her expensive suede pumps. As the shoe floated in the air, the best-of-Broadway packed crowd offered polite applause and headed for the bar en masse. Yancey, her face covered with embarrassment, looked at Basil and mouthed, "I'm going to the little girls' room."

"Are you alright?" he asked. Yancey didn't answer as she gave him a peck on his cheek and grabbed her silk beaded purse from a nearby table and rushed toward the stairs. Basil looked around the hall to make sure Campbell and Cade were okay, only to find Cade intently focused on a plateful of golden pineapple slices, honeydew melon, and chocolate-covered strawberries. Basil was smiling to himself when he heard a recognizable voice in his ear. "So you're really gonna do this?" He turned to his left and saw Monty sipping a glass of champagne.

"Did Yancey invite you?" Basil demanded.

"No, I came with a friend. She was in *Fosse* with your bride-to-be."

"Where's your man?"

"We're on a bit of a hiatus."

Basil pulled one of his business cards from his wallet and then a pen from the inside pocket of his jacket. He jotted down a number on the back of the card, and with a sly smile he whispered into Monty's ear, "Call me in a couple of weeks. I might have something for you."

"So Santa Claus is still gonna be handing out gifts in January. How wonderful," Monty said quietly. He stuck the card into the front pocket of his tight-fitting leather pants. Basil didn't respond. He noticed Cade had finished his fruit, so he headed toward the table.

YANCEY reached the bottom of the stairs, descending into darkness and then into a well-lit, flowery-fragranced bathroom that reminded her of her dressing room in Las Vegas. Yancey was looking into the mirror checking her makeup when she heard a familiar voice say, "I will remember this party for the rest of my life." Yancey looked up and saw a beaming Windsor standing a few inches from her. She was wearing an elegant dusky-gray pants suit and a pale pink sweater.

"So, you're having fun?" Yancey asked as she dabbed her lips with a tissue.

"Yes, this is great. My folks had so much fun that they left about fifteen minutes ago," Windsor said. "They wanted to rest for the wedding."

"Can you believe Ava?" Yancey asked, turning to face Windsor.

"It looks like she's having fun too," Windsor said. She smiled at Yancey and placed a strand of Yancey's hair back in place in a very big-sister moment.

"Are you always so happy?" Yancey asked.

"I don't think I've ever had a bad day in my life. If I did, I didn't know it," Windsor answered confidently.

"How can that be? Everybody has bad days."

"I have a little help from above. My family and work make me happy. And when they fail, I turn to my library of Iyanla Vanzant books."

"Who is that?"

"You're kidding, right?"

"No, who is this Vanzant person?"

"You've never heard of *Acts of Faith* or *In the Meantime*?"

"No."

"So now I know what to get the girl who has everything for Christmas." Windsor smiled.

"You think that will help me?"

"I know so. But you've got to read them," Windsor said. She locked her arm in Yancey's and moved toward the door, then said, "Now let's go enjoy the rest of your party."

AS the party came to a close and the guests began to file out, Yancey pulled a few of the flowers from the assortment of fresh pink and white roses. She decided that she would take a piece of the evening with her, and roses always brought her a small amount of joy.

Yancey was looking around the room for Ava and Basil when she suddenly heard a female voice say, "You look beautiful tonight. I don't know how you're going to top it on your wedding day." It was Darla.

"You're so sweet. When did you get here? I got the message you were running late," Yancey said as she gave her a hug.

"I got here right before your mother's toast. After she got through singing, I looked around for you. I'm sorry about being late. Our flight was two hours behind schedule and then when I got here, I had to do some last-minute Santa Claus shopping for Mollie."

"Where is Mollie? I want to see her."

"She's with my relatives in the Bronx. She told me to tell you hi and she can't wait for the wedding."

"That's sweet," Yancey said. Darla noticed she looked distracted and sad.

"Are you okay?"

"Oh, I'm fine."

"I've got some good news." She gave Yancey a supportive smile.

"What?"

"The dresses fit Mollie and me perfectly."

"That's great. Look, Darla, I've got to go find my
mother. I'm kind of worried about her. I've never seen her
drink like she did tonight." Yancey's eyes scanned the
room.

"Do you need me to help you find her?"

"No, I'll be fine. I guess she's nervous like me," Yancey
said and kissed Darla on the cheek. When Yancey pulled
back, Darla's smile was even bigger as she looked over
Yancey's shoulders. When she turned to see what had
captured Darla's attention, she saw Basil holding her
mink coat.

"I believe this belongs to you," he said. Yancey
stretched her arms out and Basil gently put the coat
around her shoulders. "Are you ready to say good-bye?"

"Did you see Darla?" Yancey asked.

"Yeah, we spent some time visiting. I'm the one who
told her where you were."

"Okay, you love bugs. I've got to go and I'll see you
early Sunday," Darla said. She hugged them both and
headed to the coat check.

"Have you seen Ava?" Yancey asked.

"She's in the limo, waiting on you."

"So you're sure you're okay with us spending Christmas apart?"

"I'm cool. I'm going to have my hands full entertaining
my family. You and Ava enjoy your time at the spa."

"You promise this is the last Christmas I will spend

alone?" Yancey asked in the voice of a little girl. Her gaze went inward, then focused on Basil's face more tightly.

"I'll do the best I can," Basil responded.

Basil and Yancey walked through the double doors and out into the night. The air was shockingly cold and the full moon looked painted in the sky. When Basil spotted Ava's car, he turned toward Yancey and said, "Well, this is it."

They squeezed each other tightly, and then Yancey looked up into his eyes and asked, "Do I deserve all this love?" An intimacy had crept into her voice.

"Only you can answer that," Basil said, wondering if his voice was giving away his true feelings. Yancey smiled at him and he returned a complicated smile of both anger and sadness. He buttoned the top of his leather coat as though he were protecting himself from the melancholy of a doomed love affair. Basil hoped spring would come soon and his sadness would be as rare as identical snowflakes.

Yancey gave him a quick peck on the lips. She was getting ready to tell him she loved him when she heard Ava's voice screaming from the backseat of the limo. She was exhausted and intoxicated. "Yancey, you gonna have the rest of your life to kiss him. Come on and git in this car. I'm tired."

Basil looked at Ava and then at Yancey and said, "Your mother's right. You should listen to her."

CHRISTMAS DAY was usually a lonely time for Yancey. She could never shake the feeling of abandonment she'd felt from spending so many Christmases without a real family. And this year it was no different, even though she was getting married the next day. She couldn't help feeling an overwhelming sadness.

Ava had ordered a six-course meal to be served in a lush suite at the Peninsula Hotel. During the serving of the soup and salad, Ava chatted endlessly about the marvelous job she had done with the engagement party. The mere sound of her voice began to grate on Yancey's nerves.

As Yancey picked at her food, she thought about calling Basil *and* Derrick. She was anxious to find out how Madison was on Christmas Day. The only thing that prevented Yancey from making either call was the certainty of a screaming tirade from Ava. Yancey knew exactly what Ava would say. She'd start off by railing against Madison and how she needed to forget about her once and for all. Then Ava would tell Yancey how expensive the wedding and engagement party were and that she couldn't continue to support her and that with Yancey's mediocre talents a rich husband was the only way she'd ever live in the style she wanted. Yancey was beginning to think that marrying Basil would be the only way to release herself from needing Ava in her life.

When the main course was served, Yancey suddenly lost her appetite. After one bite of the braised lamb, she put her fork down and looked across the table at Ava and asked, "Did you ever consider giving me up for adoption?"

"What?" Ava asked.

"You heard me. Did you ever think of giving me up?"

"What kind of fool-ass question is that?"

"Then answer it," Yancey demanded.

"Are you thinking about that little girl again?"

"Ava, her name is Madison."

"I'm not going to tell you again. Forget about her. Do you know how many men walk away from their children every day? Millions."

"I'm not talking about anyone else. I'm talking about you."

Ava didn't answer Yancey, she just continued eating. A few minutes passed and Yancey asked another question. "Do you love me?" This time Ava had a question, and an answer.

"Do I love you? I love you the best I know how. It's hard to love when nobody has ever shown you how," Ava said.

"What do you mean? Grandma loved you."

"I don't think so. Have you ever wondered why I gave you Bobby Earl Braxton's last name instead of my last name? Even though your father made it perfectly clear he wasn't the marrying kind and didn't really know if he loved me.

"I hoped, no, I *prayed* that if you didn't have my name, then maybe your life might be different. Maybe giving you up for adoption would have assured that, but when your own mother asks you—after I'd already been embarrassed in our small town—if I was sure Bobby Earl was the daddy . . . Well . . . maybe now you understand how I feel about loving anyone," Ava said.

Yancey wasn't certain but she thought she noticed tears forming in Ava's eyes. Ava took her linen napkin and dabbed the corners of her eyes while looking down. Yancey thought about what her mother had said about love, never really knowing if she had ever been loved. Yancey had felt that way the majority of her life. Until she met Basil. Since he'd also grown up without a mother, she'd sensed an immediate mutual bond, and felt he understood her. Somewhere in her heart she knew that despite his secrets he loved her. Maybe, Yancey thought, she could change Basil once and for all—she could save him with great sex and he could teach her to love. Maybe this was the reason she needed to marry Basil—she could accept his love and at the same time maybe she could learn to love. If she learned the secrets of true love, then maybe she could share them with Ava. She looked across the table at her mother, and for the first time felt sorry for her.

"Well, girl, you really know how to lift up the holiday spirit," Ava said as she got up from the table. "I need to call my husband and Hector."

I T WAS Christmas evening, and I was sitting at the bar with Campbell, when she said between sips of her hot chocolate, "For someone getting married tomorrow, you don't look happy, big brother."

"We've only really known each other for three years and you think you can read my mind?" I teased. I wondered what my face was giving away.

"Come on, aren't you excited?" Campbell playfully punched my left shoulder.

"Not really," I said slowly. "Maybe there isn't going to be a wedding." I stood up and walked over to look out the window and realized the few flakes of snow had become flurries, falling in a mood similar to my own, heavy, yet calm. It had been a good Christmas Day spent watching Cade open all the presents Campbell, Hewitt, and I had bought for him. Hewitt had taken Cade to the movies while Campbell and I had put up leftovers and loaded dishes in the dishwasher.

"What? What was going on two nights ago at your engagement party? And if that party was any indication of what the wedding is going to be like, then I know it's going to be a fantastic day. You just got the day-before jitters."

I didn't speak for a few moments. I was just staring at Campbell, trying to listen to the silence. *Maybe this isn't the best place to break the news to her,* I thought. Finally I took both of Campbell's hands and said, "Sweetheart, I'm not going to marry Yancey. I don't want you and Cade to show up at the hotel tomorrow."

"Come on now! What are you talking about? I was teasing about you not looking happy. Wasn't that you and Yancey toasting each other a couple of days ago? Didn't I see you kiss her several times?"

She was right. I had gone along with the big production Yancey and her mother had planned. I had kissed her gently several times, but my kisses were without the passion I once felt.

"You know Yancey is an actress; well, that night, I was an actor as well," I said, explaining my earlier actions.

"I don't understand what's going on. Cade is so excited about being in your wedding. I had to tell him why he couldn't go on the honeymoon with you guys."

I took a deep breath and began to say the words that had been locked in my head the past few days.

"There are some things about myself I don't like."

"We all have things we don't like about ourselves. That's what makes us human," Campbell said.

"Some of those things are pretty big, and even though I know you love me, well, I'm just not ready to share them with anyone right now. Do you understand?"

"I do."

"I hope you won't be ashamed of me when I tell you some of the things I did," I said.

"I promise," Campbell said softly.

I didn't know where to start. Was I going to place the blame on Yancey and her mother or would I tell her about my dual life? What was the real reason I wasn't going to marry Yancey? It was only twelve hours before the wedding was scheduled, and I still didn't know the truth that was driving me to leave Yancey standing at the altar alone. Suddenly, my silk tie felt tight, so I unbuttoned my collar and loosened it. I needed air. I had to get the words out.

I started by telling Campbell about seeing Yancey and Derrick in her dressing room. I then told her of my suspicions and installing the recorder. Her eyes suddenly looked larger and concerned. When I told her Yancey had a child she hadn't told me about, I thought Campbell was going to fall off the bar stool she was sitting on. I decided then I wouldn't tell her what Yancey had discovered about my past.

"Where is the child?"

"She lives with Derrick, and Yancey has never seen her."

"So that's why you're not going to marry Yancey?"

"Partly. Yancey doesn't want the child she had . . . in fact, she doesn't want children. You know how badly I want children," I said.

"I know, and you'll have them," Campbell said as she gently placed her delicate hand on top of mine and gave me a slow smile.

I told her about Yancey and Ava's plan to go after my money and spoil my chances at the Hall of Fame. I didn't think she was really in love with me, but was going to take the money and keep her former boyfriend and their child quiet. It was while I was talking about Yancey and her plans when it hit me. Why I couldn't marry Yancey.

"Are you upset because she didn't tell you about her daughter?"

I suddenly thought about my own mother and her decision to leave me with my father and I said, "No. I'm mad because she doesn't want to be a mother to this little girl. I mean, what kind of woman could just leave her child?"

Campbell didn't answer. She sat there quietly, tapping the spoon against her mug. When she finally looked up, I could tell her eyes were misted with tears. I realized that we were both thinking not about Yancey, but our own mother. I wanted to say, "I'm sorry for my insensitive question," but Campbell was looking toward the window as snow continued to fall. I took a sip of my coffee, which was now cold and watery.

"It still hurts a great deal, doesn't it?" Campbell asked.

"What?"

"Mother leaving you."

"No. I mean, she did what she had to do," I said as the words "mother leaving you" echoed through my mind. For a second I didn't know who I hated more—my mother or Yancey. Then I hated myself for wanting the love of these two women so badly, knowing full well it was impossible for each of them to love without limits.

"She felt her life was in danger," Campbell said, interrupting my negative thoughts.

"My pops wouldn't ever raise his hand to a woman," I said defensively.

"Look, Basil, neither one of us knows what happened in their relationship. I'm sure they were both good people who made some mistakes. But you can't let their mistakes guide your life. We have to learn from their mistakes," Campbell said in a consoling voice.

"Do you think our mother ever regretted leaving me?"

"I'm certain not a day went by when she didn't think of you," she said confidently.

"How do you know that?"

"I know. After she told me about you we talked about you almost every day. I know she regretted her decision."

"I remember you told me how much she talked about me before she died. Trust me, I didn't mean anything about what kind of woman would give up her child. And even though I never knew our mother I know she was not the kind of woman Yancey has turned out to be. Look what a great job she did in raising you."

Campbell gave me a sweet smile and then asked, "Do you love Yancey?"

"I don't know how I feel. All I know is that her actions have hurt me and made the mistrust I have for women return. It took a little vacation, but it's back. I also feel humiliated, and I hope when Yancey comes down the aisle and I leave the moment she gets to the altar, leave her standing there alone . . . well, I just want to see her face."

"Is that going to make you feel better?"

"Yeah," I said quickly.

"Basil, please don't do that. If you don't want to marry Yancey, that's okay, but take the high road here. Just tell her why you can't marry her. Don't make a fool out of her in front of all her friends."

"Didn't I tell you? Yancey doesn't have any friends. Those people who will be sitting there are her fans, her subjects."

Campbell reached her hands over to clasp mine. She looked directly in my eyes and said, "If you're hurt or humiliated, it will pass. Trust me. If you just sit down and write your feelings tonight or tomorrow morning . . . Write how you feel about Yancey, Mother, and suddenly meeting a sister and nephew you didn't know about. If that doesn't help, go back to professional help, especially if you think we, the people who love you, don't understand your pain. Years from now you'll look back and see how much you've grown from this experience. Don't worry, Yancey will have to face up to her past sooner or later. If she doesn't, her future will be torture." I saw affection in Campbell's eyes but also a sadness. A sadness that I was causing with my vengeful heart. That made me sad too, and I was hoping the tears hiding in the corner of my eyes wouldn't betray my masculine ego. I couldn't shed tears even in front of my sister.

A long moment passed and we looked at each other in heavy silence just holding hands. I knew Campbell was right. Yet I didn't know what to say to make us feel better. Maybe I *could* write the pain away.

AVA WAS walking out of the bathroom of Yancey's suite patting her hair in place when she realized Yancey had not moved since she left the room. She was sitting on the edge of the bed in her slip, staring quietly out the window.

"Didn't I tell you to get ready? We got a party to preside over," Ava said. She was dressed wedding-ready in an ivory satin corset and silver ball gown.

"I'm not going to any party. Didn't you hear anything I said? There is not going to be a wedding."

"That may well be true, but I'm not going to let it stop the party I've planned. So let me tell you again. Put on that wedding dress, call the makeup guy, and let's get started. We will deal with Basil later," Ava said.

"Why do you think he's not going to marry me?" Yancey asked.

"I don't know for certain, but if I find out you messed

this up by telling him . . . well, you're going to have to deal with me and that ain't going to be pretty. Especially after all the money I've spent."

"I didn't tell him anything," Yancey said.

"Then you have nothing to worry about. The only person who should fear me is Mr. John Basil Henderson. I've already told my press person to arrange a press conference right after the new year. We will give Basil forty-eight hours to meet my demands and if he doesn't, then we go to the press."

"Why don't we just cut our losses and leave him alone?" Yancey pleaded.

"*Our* losses? What have you lost?"

Before Yancey could answer, there was a knock at the door. "Maybe it's Basil," Yancey said. "Maybe he's changed his mind," she added as she raced toward the door.

"Yancey, don't answer that door," Ava screamed. It was too late. When Yancey flung open the door, there stood Basil, his gray eyes icy and intense.

Yancey rushed toward him and threw her arms around him, then whispered, "I knew you wouldn't let me down. I love you." Basil was holding a journal in his hands and stood like a stone statue.

Ava moved toward them and pulled Yancey away from Basil. Then she started screaming at him, "You've fucked with the wrong woman, you sick mutherfucker. When we get through with you, you're gonna regret the day you were born."

Basil ignored Ava's tirade. His eyes were fixed on Yancey, who stood mercifully silent. She could tell from the look in his eyes that he hadn't changed his mind. She just wanted to know why he had decided not to marry her.

Ava kept talking even though both Basil and Yancey were ignoring her. "You can forget about the Hall of Fame. When we finish our press conference, you're going to be the laughingstock of the sports world. Do you think parents are going to let their sons sign with a freak like you?"

Then, in an emotionless voice, he held the journal toward Yancey and said, "I want you to have this. Maybe it will explain why we ended up this way."

This is not happening, Yancey began to say to herself over and over. Her eyes were brimming with tears. She moved closer to Basil and began to speak slowly, with hopeful pauses, her voice trembling. "We don't have to get married today . . . We can wait . . . Whatever you're going through, I will be here for you . . . I know about you and men . . . I can help you." She folded her hands over her chest and dropped her head.

"I'm going to leave now," Basil said.

"Don't leave me," Yancey said, her face now wet with tears.

"Yancey, stop it! Stop begging this sick faggot to stay. We will get him."

Yancey turned toward Ava and screamed, "Shut up! Stop it! I should never have listened to you!"

Basil focused his eyes on Ava and shook his head. He then reached into his jacket pocket and pulled out a tape. "Ava, before you schedule your press conference, I think you should listen to this. Just so you know, I have a copy for your husband as well. I'll be sure to use the delivery service you like so much. What's his name? Is it Hector?"

"Get out . . . get out!" Ava yelled. She moved toward Basil and started hitting his chest with her hands balled. Basil firmly moved her hands away, pushed her back, and gave Yancey a mournful glance. He then left the room without a good-bye.

Yancey turned her back toward Ava and picked up the journal Basil had left. She noticed that "Basil and Yancey" was embossed on the front cover and moved her fingers across the words slowly. She opened the journal to the first page and started reading.

Dear Yancey,
I want to save you from the world. I want you to save me from myself. I had other plans for this journal and you. I wanted it to be a history of our love story. But you and I both know you can't have a love story when there is only one person in love.

"What does that say?" Ava asked. She moved toward Yancey and tried to pull the journal from her hands. But Yancey closed the journal and refused to let it loose.

"Let me have it!" Ava demanded.

Yancey continued to hold the journal tightly to her chest. She stared at Ava with eyes shining with tears and said, "I want you out of here right now."

"I'm not leaving until you let me see what's in that journal," Ava said firmly.

"This journal is addressed to me and you will never read a word. Now leave. I want to be alone."

"Oh, you can be alone. Sit here by yourself and wallow in a pity party. As for me, I got a real party to host. We can't let all those guests and the publicity go to waste. When I get back to Beverly Hills, I'll send you a bill for all this wedding shit." Ava looked at herself in the mirror and grabbed her small handbag.

She was on her way out the door when Yancey asked, "If I pay the bill, will you promise to leave me alone? Forever?"

Ava stared at her in silence and then said, "Only if your check clears."

T HE D'AWG is back!

You didn't think I was going to let those two demented divas have the last word, did you? On the evening I was supposed to get married, I boarded a plane in the first-class section bound for Montego Bay, Jamaica. I played a lot of golf, went snorkeling, and roamed the beaches like a cell phone. I ate some fantastic seafood, did some dancing at a reggae club. I made love with a beautiful Jamaican sistah on the beach and did the bump and grind with an equally beautiful Jamaican man with shoulder-length dreads on the terrace of the villa I rented. A good time was had by all. I only thought about Yancey about four times a day. What was she doing? Did she read the journal? Did she realize how much I had loved her? Who would be her next victim?

I did a lot of thinking as I strolled the beaches. What was I supposed to learn from my experience with Yancey?

I thought about some of the women and men I had hurt with my own selfishness. I remembered the wise words of a New York cab driver who once told me, "Life is full of required courses; it's the electives that are a bitch." I guess Yancey was an elective for me. Being in love with her was like taking a course in nuclear physics when my major was basket weaving. But I know I'm a hard course as well.

When I got back to New York, I discovered one of my clients had given me two tickets to the Super Bowl for a Christmas present. I started to take Cade, but since I was in party mode, I decided to take another route. I invited Raymond, Zurich, Monty, and Rosa, a honey I met on the flight back from Jamaica. I decided whoever said yes first would be the one I might consider for another course in one of life's toughest lessons: love. So I'm waiting. I know I won't be going alone, because I told each of them to call me on my private line if they wanted to join me. I checked this morning and there are three messages. I'll listen to them in a couple of days.

In the meantime I will issue a warning to all the mothers and fathers out there. Tell your sons and daughters. I'm back, in full form. And I'm out there. Roamin'. And switching lanes . . .